The Dreadful Fate of Jonathan York

A Yarn for the Strange at Heart

by Kory Merritt

Andrews McMeel
Publishing®

Kansas City • Sydney • London

Lo! HARK! Listen! ...and BEWARE!

Beware Pen-tip Polishers
and Ditto Wranglers.

Beware planbook toters, wristwatch warblers,
armchair denizens.

Beware those of the daily routine,
who take their lunch at noon on the dot
and never use the spicy mustard,
for fear of cramps and belly-bloating.

Beware those of the spotless yard,
who never dare venture
beyond the dyed grass and trimmed hedges
to The Lost Side of Suburbia,
where tree roots dance the Twist
and lichen glimmers and brooks burble
bad poetry.

Beware ye of little nerve,
for there is a Story out there,
lurking in the brambles,

and it knows your name.

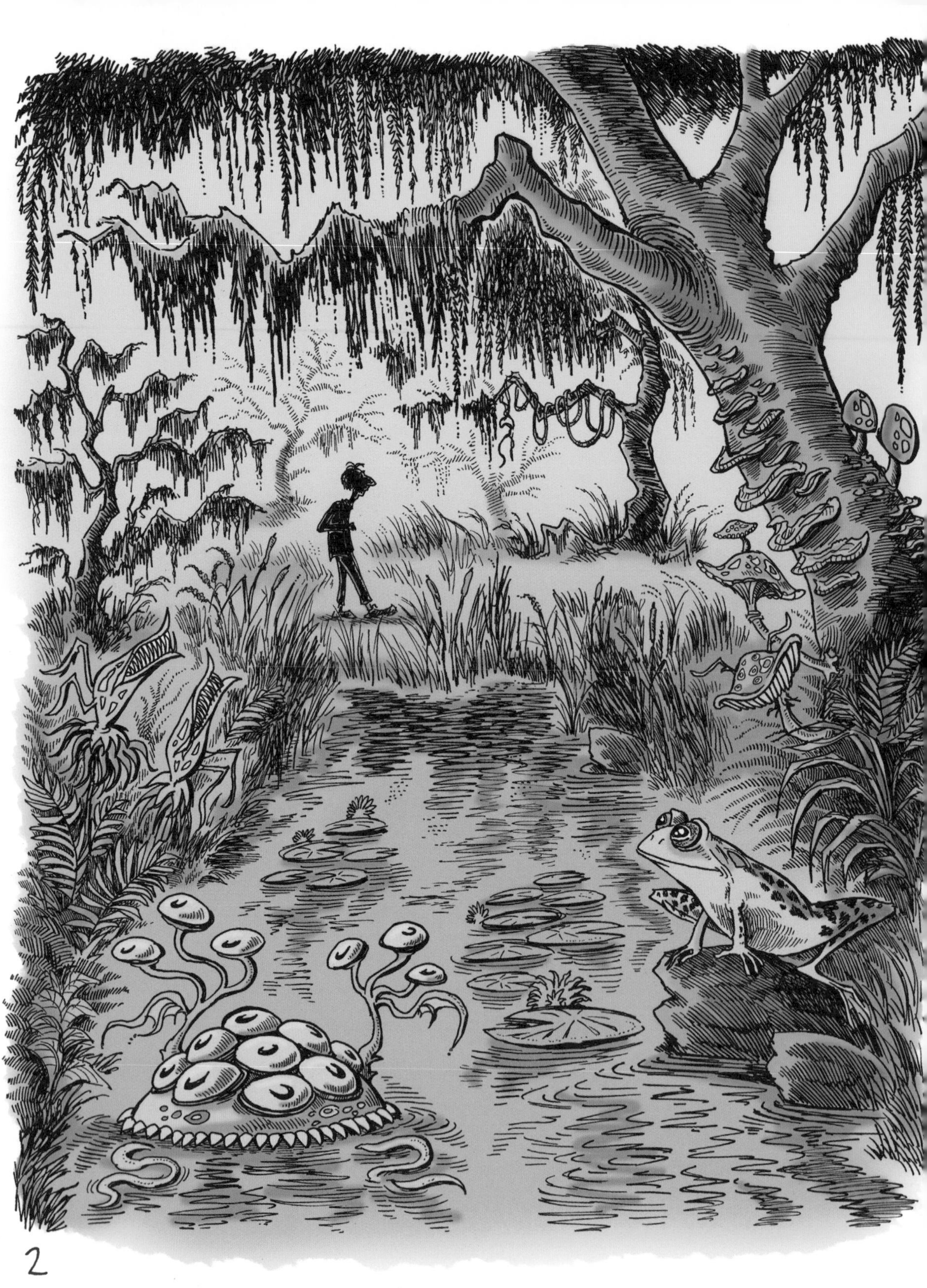

Jonathan YORK was LOST...

Lost in the gloom of a wilderness he had never experienced before, and had hoped he would never experience at all.

Poor, poor Mr. York. The shortcut through the swamp had seemed like a good idea in the afternoon, but that was when the sun was bright in the late summer sky. *NOW*? *NOW* was different. The sun was sinking, and the evening shadows had sidled in like predators seeking out the sick animals in a herd.

3

A toad hopped into the middle
of the path and stared at Mr. York
with stern golden eyes.
Mr. York stopped and stared back.

"What have I done to deserve
this dreadful fate?" he asked
the toad. "I've always been such
a harmless fellow. Truly I have.
I was splendidly behaved as a child,
and pleasantly well-mannered when
I attended Brockleport Community College."

He crouched down to the toad's level, and
when he spoke again his voice reached the pit
of an actor in a podunk theater troupe.

"So why? Why must a mild person
such as me, a humble clerk at the
Brockleport General Store, be doomed
to wander this accursed swamp?"

4

The toad blinked and hopped into the undergrowth. Mr. York stood and glanced around sheepishly. Lost a few hours and already he was talking to amphibians.

It was getting darker, and a steady drizzle was sifting through the canopy. Mr. York shuddered. His chances of finding his way out of the swamp before nightfall seemed slimmer by the minute.

Just as the last of the daylight fizzled he heard something on the path ahead.

Footsteps! And, judging by the sound, more than one set!

His neck prickled. He wasn't sure if he should run hopefully *toward* the footsteps or frantically *away* from them.

In the end he didn't run at all—he simply stayed rooted where he stood, unable to make up his mind as the strangers emerged from the shadows.

There were three of them, and Mr. York was relieved to see they at least *looked* human enough. One was a woman of medium height clad in a hooded robe. Another was a tall, gangly man with wild hair. The third was... *odd*, to say the least.

Mr. York raised his hand in a meager half-wave.

"Hello. My name is Jonathan York." His voice cracked as he spoke.

The hooded woman waved back. "Nice to meet you, Mr. York."

Mr. York swallowed. His throat clicked.

"I don't wish to trouble you, but I'm lost, you see, and I should very much like to find my way out of the swamp before it gets too dark."

The lanky fellow shook his head. "No such luck, Mr. York. Your best bet is to spend the night at the Cankerbury Inn and get a fresh start in the morning."

"The Cankerbury Inn? Where's that?"

"Down the trail a bit," said the hooded woman. "We're heading there now. You're welcome to join us."

Mr. York heaved a sigh of relief. He wasn't too keen on staying in some inn with a gaggle of strangers, but it was certainly better than wandering the darkness of an alien swamp.

The party moved onward, walking single file and never speaking. Mr. York plodded along behind them, his head down and his hands jammed into his pockets.

The swamp was now alive with the sounds of its nocturnal denizens. Some noises were familiar: the rasping of katydids, the chorus of treefrogs, the lonesome call of a nightjar... but mixed in were voices Mr. York did not recognize: guttural groans and shrieks and growls, sinister hisses and gurgles and snarls. He was glad to be traveling with a group.

The party stopped abruptly, and the hooded woman pointed to a smaller overgrown trail snaking off the main path. Through the trees they could see a light.

8

They took the smaller trail and soon found a clearing, in the center of which s a weathered old house. The shingles were cracked and warped, and rain had stripped the paint away years ago.

They approached the door, and the hooded woman gave a timid knock. answer. She knocked again, this time harder. Still no answer. Finally, after e third knock, there was a shuffling sound, and the door creaked open.

9

A little old man squinted out at them.
He scrunched his face and
adjusted the spectacles
perched on his nose. He held
a lantern, which he thrust
forward, almost offensively.

"Yes?" he asked in a
voice as creaky as the door.
"What do you want?"

The hooded woman dipped her
body in what may have been a curtsy.

"We beg your pardon, good sir,
but is this not the Cankerbury Inn?"

The old man scratched—or possibly *picked*—the rim of his right nos
"It is. What of it?"

"Well, it's dark and raining, and my fellow travelers and I
have no desire to pass through the swamp on a night
such as this."

The old man rolled something between his fingers and flicked it aside.

So it **WASN'T** merely a scratch, thought Mr. York.
He tried not to make a face.

"And you expect me to give you each a room so you may rest your weary carcasses," grumbled the old man.

"If you please, sir," said the hooded woman.

"Huh! I dunno. There's been strange folk on the prowl lately. Nasty folk! Thieves and scoundrels. How am I to know you four won't rob me blind during the night? Perhaps you're even in cahoots with that awful West Bleekport Gang!"

The lanky man was growing impatient.
"Are you going to give us rooms or not?"

Before the old man could give his final word, another voice answered from within the house.

"Of course we will!"

An old lady appeared behind the old man.

"And we'll be happy to do so. Won't we, Mortimer?"

The old man crinkled his face at her.

"Aye. Seems we will. As long as they pay, that is."

Panic swept through Mr. York's scrawny frame. *PAY?* It suddenly dawned on him that he was not carrying any cash.

"What's the price?" he asked. His voice cracked again, and he blushed. "I-I don't have much money with me."

"Money? What use have we for money? The wife and I have all we need in this house, plus the well for water and the coop for eggs."

"But you said there was a price."

"Aye, there is," said the old lady, "and it's something each of you can afford. But enough of that now. It's dark, and you don't want to be out in Halfrock Swamp after dark."

"Why?" Mr. York asked before he could stop himself. "What's out there?"

The old lady turned to Mr. York with a disturbing gleam in her eyes.

"Because, young man, Halfrock Swamp is a place of nightmares...

"There's Squeeveleegs and Gluggerslogs and Lackadiles!

"...there's Gigundopods and Lacerating Manti and even the All-Absorbing Shlutherglurk!

"And that's just the beginning! I won't even mention the horror that dwells on the Northeast Edge! ...Now, enough of that grim talk. Please, come into the kitchen for some supper."

She led them into a cramped kitchen and dished out bowls of lumpy stew. Mr. York might have passed on the meal under normal circumstances, but trudging through the swamp had roused his appetite. The stew tasted strange, but was somehow satisfying.

After they'd finished their dinner, the old man shuffled in and took a seat at the head of the table. He lit his pipe and sat puffing with an expression that might have meant contentment or annoyance... It was hard to read a face so scrunched.

They sat in uncomfortable silence for what seemed like an hour but was really no more than ten minutes. Finally the old man cleared his throat and spoke.

"The time has come to collect your payment. Now, as I mentioned, the wife and I have met our needs and therefore have no use for material goods. Instead, we ask you pay us in stories."

"Stories?" said the lanky man.

"Yes, stories. One per guest. We live alone out here in the swamp, and although I don't care much for company, I do enjoy listening to stories, particularly stories of adventure that take me back to my younger days, when I had many stories of my own."

Mr. York's stomach churned. *Stories?* The old man was making them pay with *stories?* Mr. York feared public speaking almost as much as he feared death and pestilence, and the thought of sharing a story with strange made cold beads of sweat pop out on his forehead

The old man continued:
"*After you tell your story, I will give you a room key, and you will be allowed to spend the night. Understand?*"

The guests nodded blankly.

"*Good. So...who's first?*"

Mr. York's heart raced. The prospect of public speaking was upsetting enough, but now new and nastier thought had revealed itself: *he could not think of a story to tell!* Nope. *Nothing.* His mind grappled for sustenance but found *nothing.* There was not a single event in Mr. York's life worth reciting.

The old man scanned the guests.

"Well ?" he repeated. "Who's first ?"

Finally the hooded woman raised her hand. Mr. York relaxed, grateful that he might have a chance to think of a story.

"My story is a true one, though I don't tell it often," said the hooded woman. She glanced around the table, avoiding eye contact with the others. "It's about a discovery I made in my childhood years. I think I was ten years old. Or twelve. Though my age doesn't really matter. What *does* matter is what I learned about the Slynderfell Ice Cream Company..."

Virginia liked her calico cats,
And flowers red and gold.
She liked her cocoa piping hot,
and iced tea freezing cold.

She liked to sit and watch the clouds,
Then drift into a dream.
But most of all Virginia loved
Slynderfell's Ice Cream.

SLYNDERFELL'S
ICE CREAM
CAVALCADE

Caramel Electra

Slynderfell's Ice Cream, Oh Yes!
A taste that can't be beat!
One lick will tantalize your tongue
and tingle to your feet.

The flavor was a cavalcade
Of sweet and tangy zest.
A symphony inside your mouth!
It simply was the best.

One day Virginia had an urge
To go and promenade
Down to town and take a tour
To see how ice cream's made.

In her head she saw the scene:
Big scoops and jumbo spoons,
And cheery elves all stirring vats
While singing merry tunes.

They'd blend and mix that magic goop
and swirl it into paste,
And serve it up to little pups,
Who then would test the taste.

She reached the gates and rang the bell
And asked to please come in.
The doors creaked open, and there she saw
A fellow, weird and thin.

"Allow me to introduce myself,"
Said the strange and zany fellow.
Do not be skitterish, don't go squid,
No need for turning yellow.

My name is Leeshkin Slynderfell,
And welcome to my keep.
It's here where we produce the cream
That sets your hearts a-leap!

"Yes," in this factory you will find
That mystastical dessert
That makes Wonka seem like cuttlefish snot
And Keebler worse than dirt.

23

"Kaloo Kaluk! Praise the nebula!
Such supoibness you will sample!
It'll blast your tastebuds to the next dimensio
And make your tum-tum ample!"

"Oh let me in!" Virginia begged.
"I've waited oh so long!
Please, O Mr. Slynderfell,
To stall me would be wrong!"

"Of course, my sweet li'l periwink,
I'll show you what's in store.
You'll soon see how we make
the cream...

...It's all behind
this door..."

24

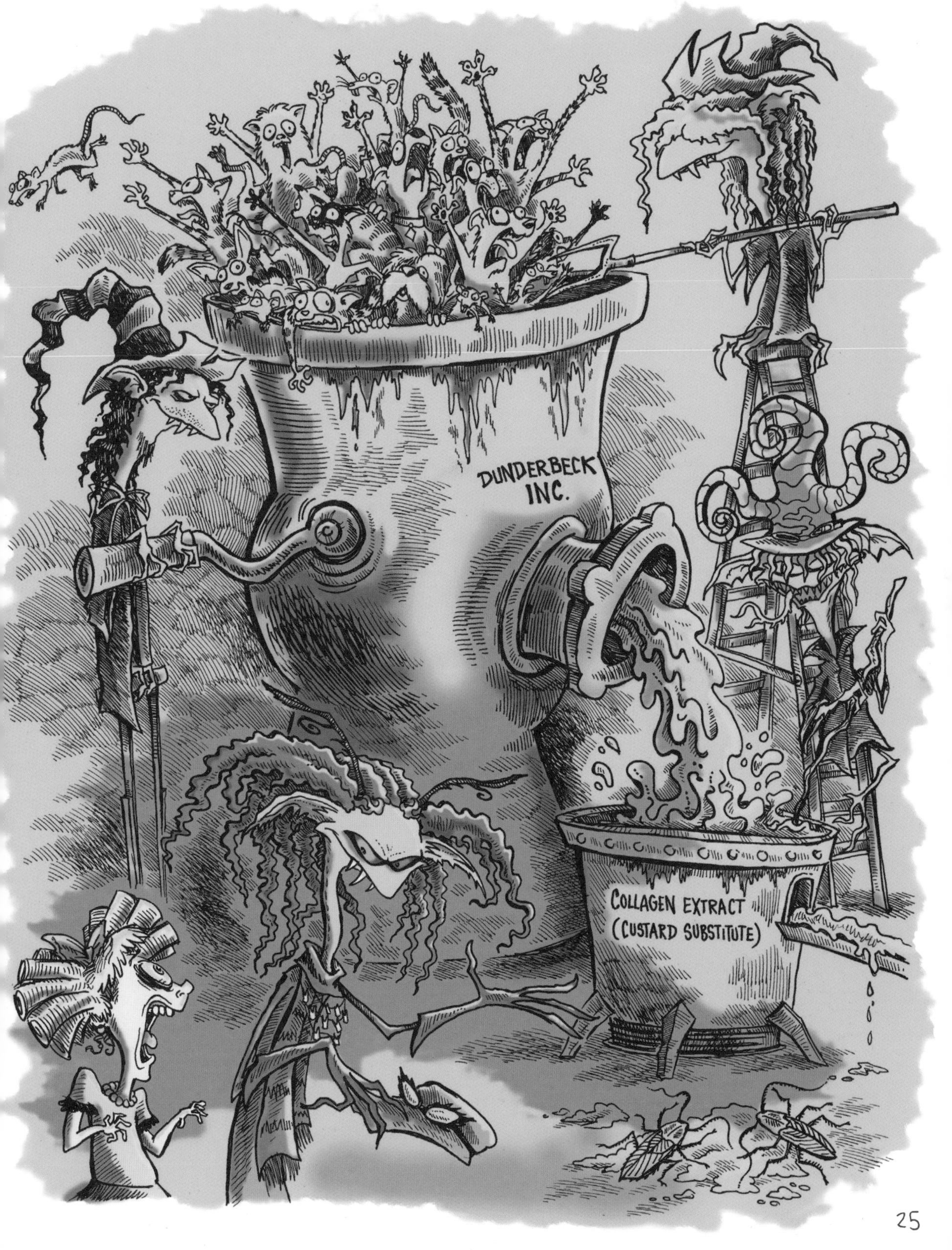
DUNDERBECK INC.
COLLAGEN EXTRACT
(CUSTARD SUBSTITUTE)

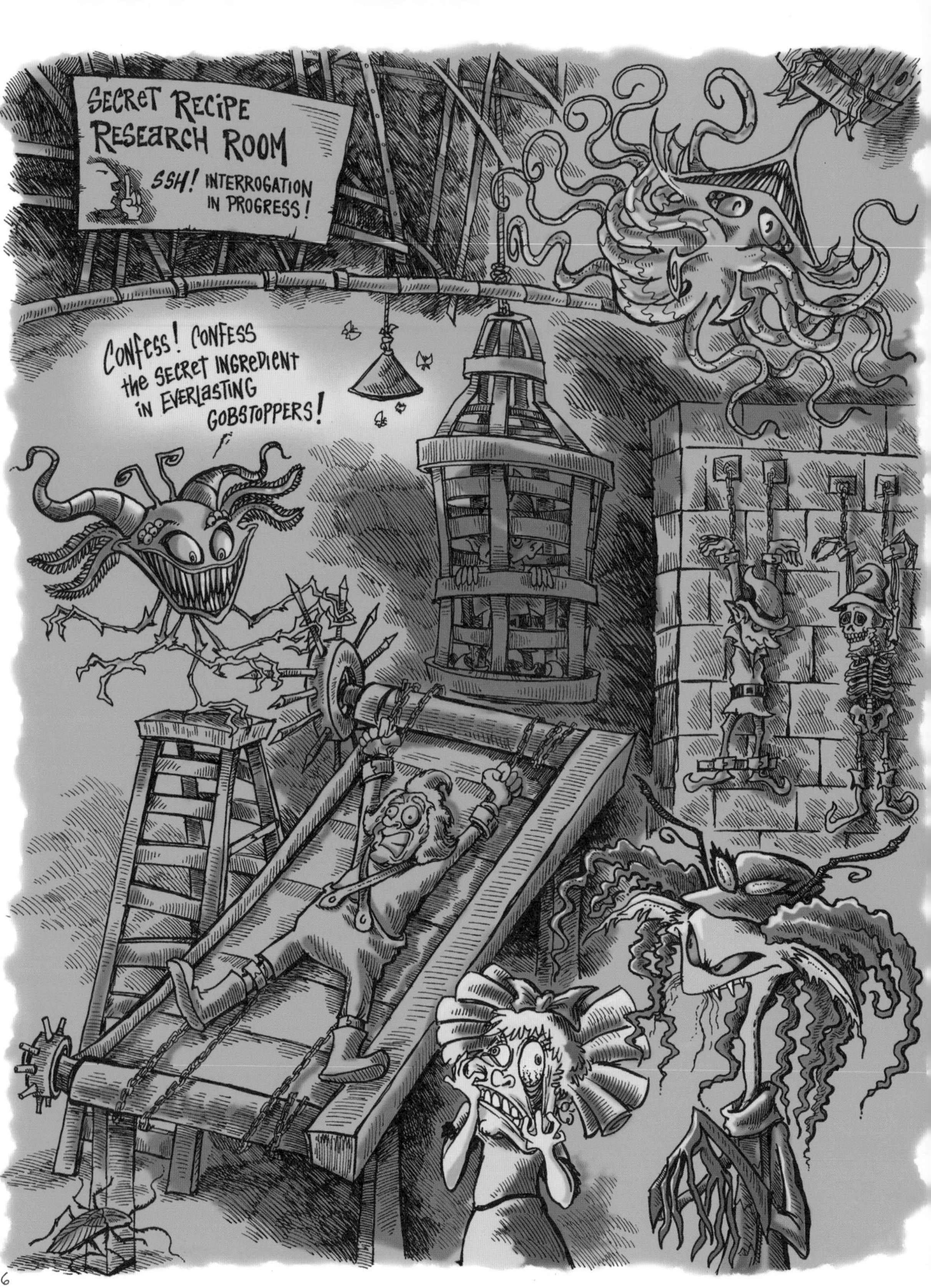
SECRET RECIPE RESEARCH ROOM
SSH! INTERROGATION IN PROGRESS!
CONFESS! CONFESS the SECRET INGREDIENT in EVERLASTING GOBSTOPPERS!

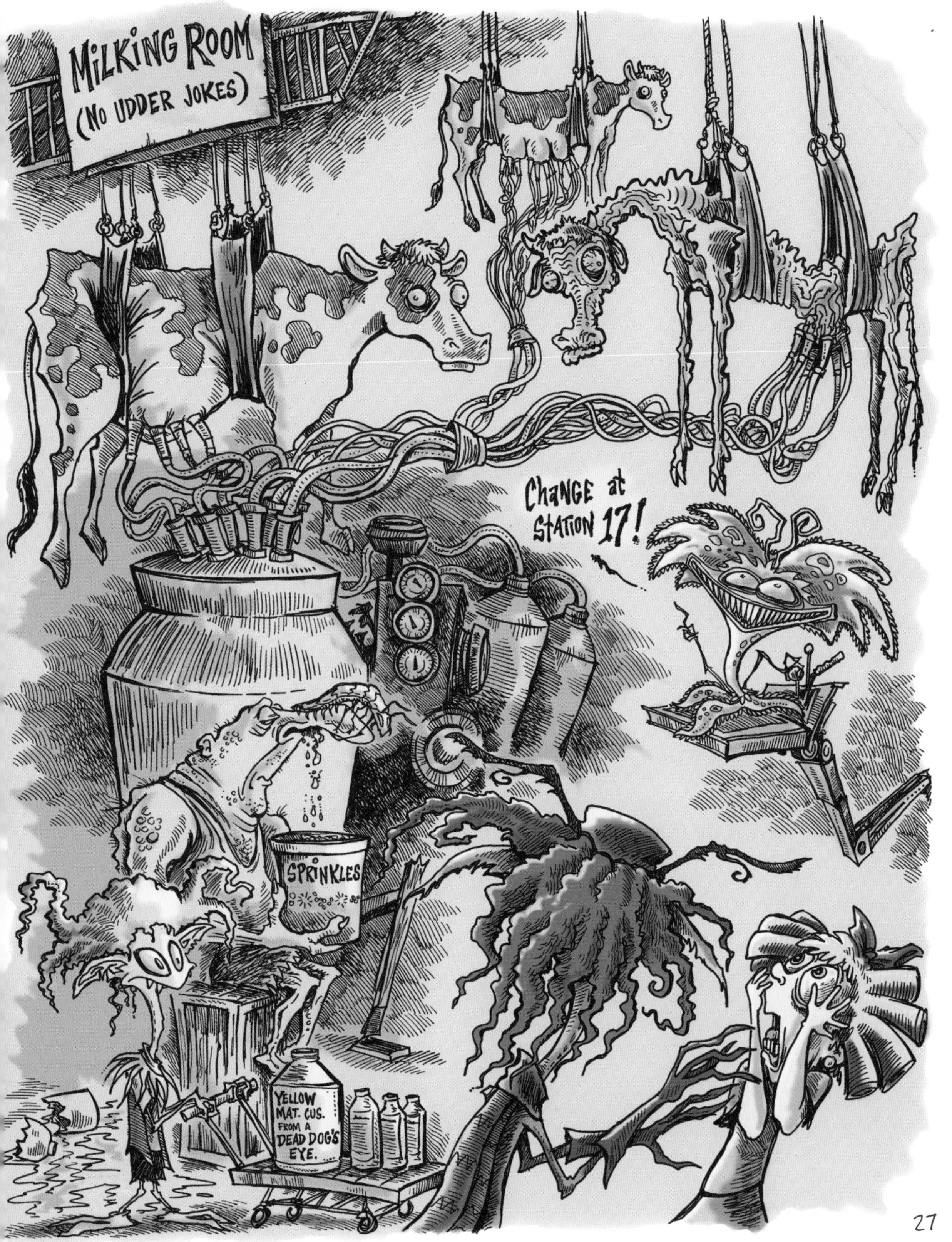
MILKING ROOM
(NO UDDER JOKES)
CHANGE at STATION 17!
SPRINKLES
YELLOW MAT. CUS. FROM A DEAD DOG'S EYE.

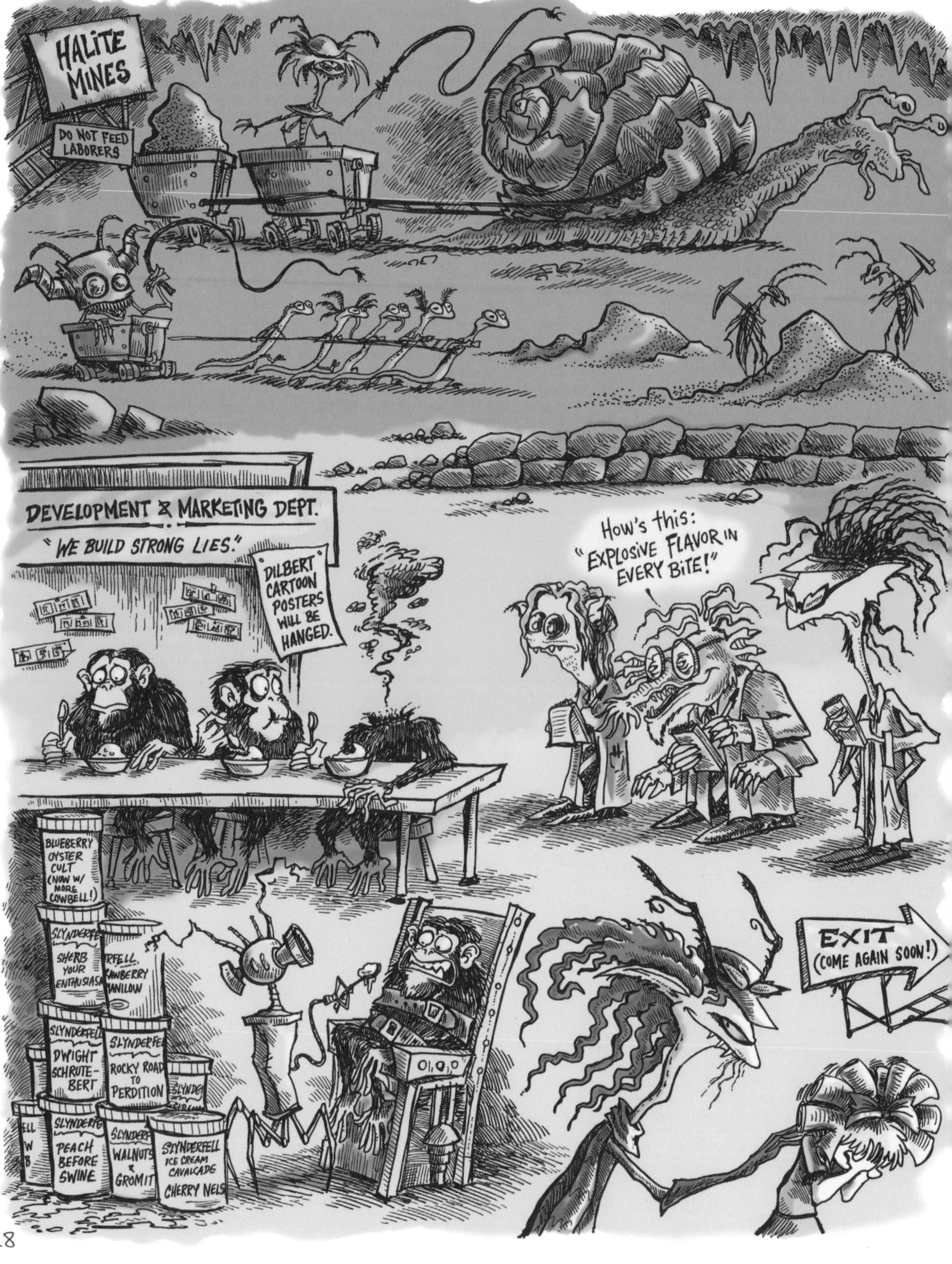
HALITE MINES
DO NOT FEED LABORERS
DEVELOPMENT & MARKETING DEPT.
"WE BUILD STRONG LIES."
DILBERT CARTOON POSTERS WILL BE HANGED.
How's this: "EXPLOSIVE FLAVOR IN EVERY BITE!"
BLUEBERRY OYSTER CULT (NOW W/ MORE COWBELL!)
SLYNDERFE
SHERB YOUR ENTHUSIASM
RFELL AWBERRY MANILOW
SLYNDERFELL
DWIGHT SCHRUTE-BERT
SLYNDERFE
ROCKY ROAD TO PERDITION
SLYNDERFE
PEACH BEFORE SWINE
SLYNDERF
WALNUTS & GROMIT
SLYNDERFELL ICE CREAM CAVALCADE
CHERRY NELS
EXIT (COME AGAIN SOON!)

By the time they reached the exit door,
Virginia was a mess;
Her face was green, her lips all blue,
She'd even wet her dress!

"And now you know how ice cream's made!
Though it may be unnerving,
I've just the thing to soothe your wits:
Another heaping serving!"

"NO!" Virginia cried aloud.
"I won't bear another bite!
I'll never eat your brand again!
It simply won't be right!"

"Oh, I think you will, in fact,"
He said with a sly grin.
"You're accustlimated to the taste,
And your stamina's worn thin.

"You human folk are all alike,
And, if I may be mean,
You'd rather send the world to heck
Than alter your routine.

"There's evil in your daily lives,
But to right it would be sour.
You might have to ride a bus to w
Or take a shorter shower!

"You hate to inconveen yourselve
You hate to sacrifice.
You know you'll never mend your w
So go on and take the ice

Virginia scowled and stomped away
Far from that awful place.
She was ashamed of what she'd seen.
O, such a cruel disgrace!

That night she still was rather ill,
And felt like she could scream...

...And so she went and
drowned her woes...

YNDERFELL
ICE CREAM
CAVALCADE
SERENITY
NOW!

...In Slynderfell's Ice Cream.

The hooded woman finished her story and looked up. Her eyes darted around the kitchen uneasily, as if she were personally responsible for the crimes of the Slynderfell Ice Cream Company (and, in a way, she was).

"Hrmph! I always knew that Slynderfell fellow was up to no good," grunted the old man. "I'll stick to the wife's Midgeweed pie, thank you."

He pulled a key from his pocket.

"This opens the first door on the left," he said, pointing to the hall.

"Have a restful night, and may your dreams be devoid of frozen desserts."

The hooded woman pounced on the key. She clutched it with both hands as she fled from the table and disappeared down the hall.

The old man leaned back and rested his hands on his stomach.

"So...Who's next?"

Once again, the realization that he had not yet thought of a story to tell threw Mr. York's mind into a frenzy. He sat perfectly still, afraid the slightest movement would attract the old man's attention.

"*I'll go,*" said the lanky man.

Though relieved, Mr. York reminded himself that he absolutely *must* think of a story before the lanky man finished his tale.

"My story is also true, though perhaps you'll find it a bit hard to swallow."

Mr. York doubted any story could be harder to swallow than the story of Slynderfell's Ice Cream.

The lanky man leaned forward, took a breath, and began...

A while ago; two years or three,
I went with my lover to the Sineligo Sea.
And while the tide came in and rose
I took a moment to propose.

Oh what a rare and joyous thing
When her eyes beheld the ring.
The ring, you see, was emerald green;
The richest stone she'd ever seen.

Alas, the joy we felt was brief;
A wave rolled in and hit the reef.
The water flew and caught her grip,
And from her grasp the ring did slip.

It dropped straight down, as I had feared,
Gave one last gleam then disappeared
Into the inky dark below.
How quick it sank? We'll never know.

Her eyes swelled up and soon broke free
With tears as salty as the sea.
She fell to knee and gasped for air;
A sight I simply could not bear!

"My dear, I'll prove my sweet devotion!
I'll save your treasure from the ocean!
For there's no phantom of the deep
That's worse than watching my girl weep!"

I took a breath and then I dove
Into the darkness of the cove...

35

Deep into that murky black,
I swam straight down, did not look back,
Passing shoals of neon zimmers,
A wall of scales that glints and shimmers.

A curious cephalopod slid by,
Then slunk away (they are quite shy).
A team of prowling sharks cruised near,
And filled my heart with gripping fear.

The deeper down I seemed to go
The darker were the depths below.
And all around that world beneath
Were things with gnashing needle-teeth!

Gulpers! Glunklers! Loathsome Anglers!
Trigglodytes and Glowthing Danglers!
And though these monsters gave their best,
They could not shake me from my quest.

And then, at last, deep in that brine,
I looked and saw a welcome shine.
Settled in the ocean floor
I spied what I had come here for.

I snatched that symbol of my love
And started for the land above.
But then with a most fearful moan,
I realized I was not alone...

'Twas a beast of awesome size,
With lance-like fangs and lightless eyes!
And now this demon from the black
Was sizing me up for a snack!

I could not spare the time to waste
To see if it would like my taste,
So for the surface I did shoot,
With the fiend in hot pursuit!

My limbs were flailing to-and-fro,
And now I feared my lungs would blow!
I was a blur, to say the least,
Yet still I could not ditch the beast!

And just when I thought I was din',
The beast gave up and let me win.
So having cheated my own death,
I reached the top and gasped for breath.

I turned and met my lover's eyes,
Then raised the arm that held the prize.
She shrieked and cheered and waved her hand
As I hauled myself to land.

She hugged me close and kissed my face,
And slipped the ring back into place.

But after a brief pause or so
She turned to me and said, "You know,
I love this stone, now that is true...

But I'd love it more if it were blue."

So here I am in a strip mall shop,
And will this haggling ever stop?
Yet to say this makes me sound so cheap:
Life was saner in the deep.

RETURNS &
EXCHANGES

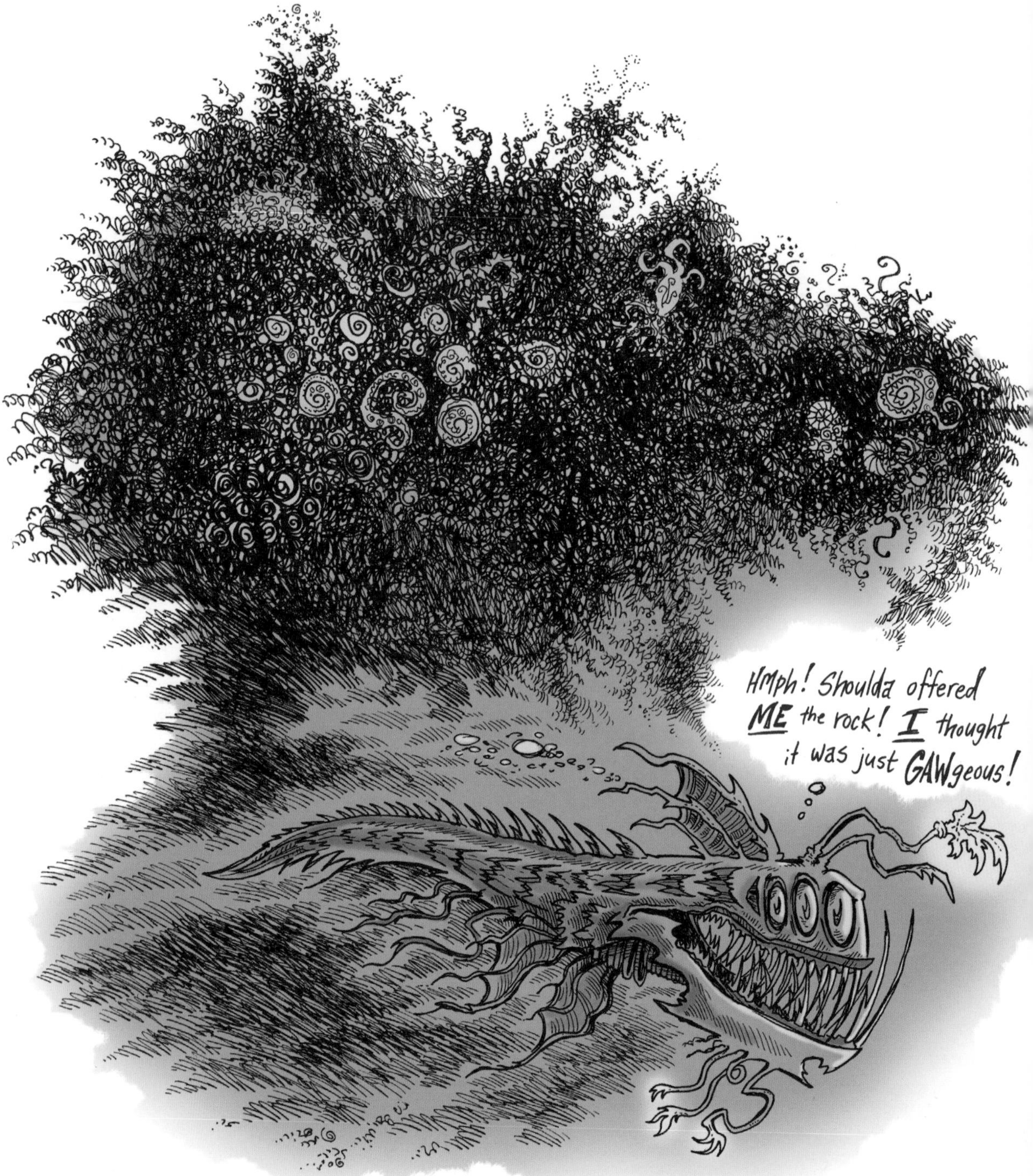
HMph! Shoulda offered ME the rock! I thought it was just GAWgeous!

The lanky man's voice trailed off. He stood and flexed his limbs.

"I suppose I can relate to that story," said the old man. "Been married ifty-odd years. Can't say there hasn't been a time here or there when I feel like jumping in the swamp and living with the scrunweed and bullfrogs."

The old man laughed heartily at his own joke. The old lady, who had been busying rself in the next room, stomped in and shook her fist.

"Chuckle away, Mortimer, 'cause won't be chucklin' when I'm ead and gone! You'll be sittin' t this table with an empty late in front of ya and a sea of dirty underwear beneath ya! And I doubt he bullfrogs'll be fixin' er meals and washin' yer shorts!"

The old man shot his wife an ugly look as he passed the lanky man a key.

"Second door on the right," he grunted.

Now that his buffer was down to only one other person, Mr. York was on the brink of full-blown panic. But despite his best efforts, he *still* could not think of a story worth telling.

The odd fellow snapped his fingers, signaling that he was ready to share his anecdote, and even before he started, Mr. York was certain that it was going to be a *weird* one...

43

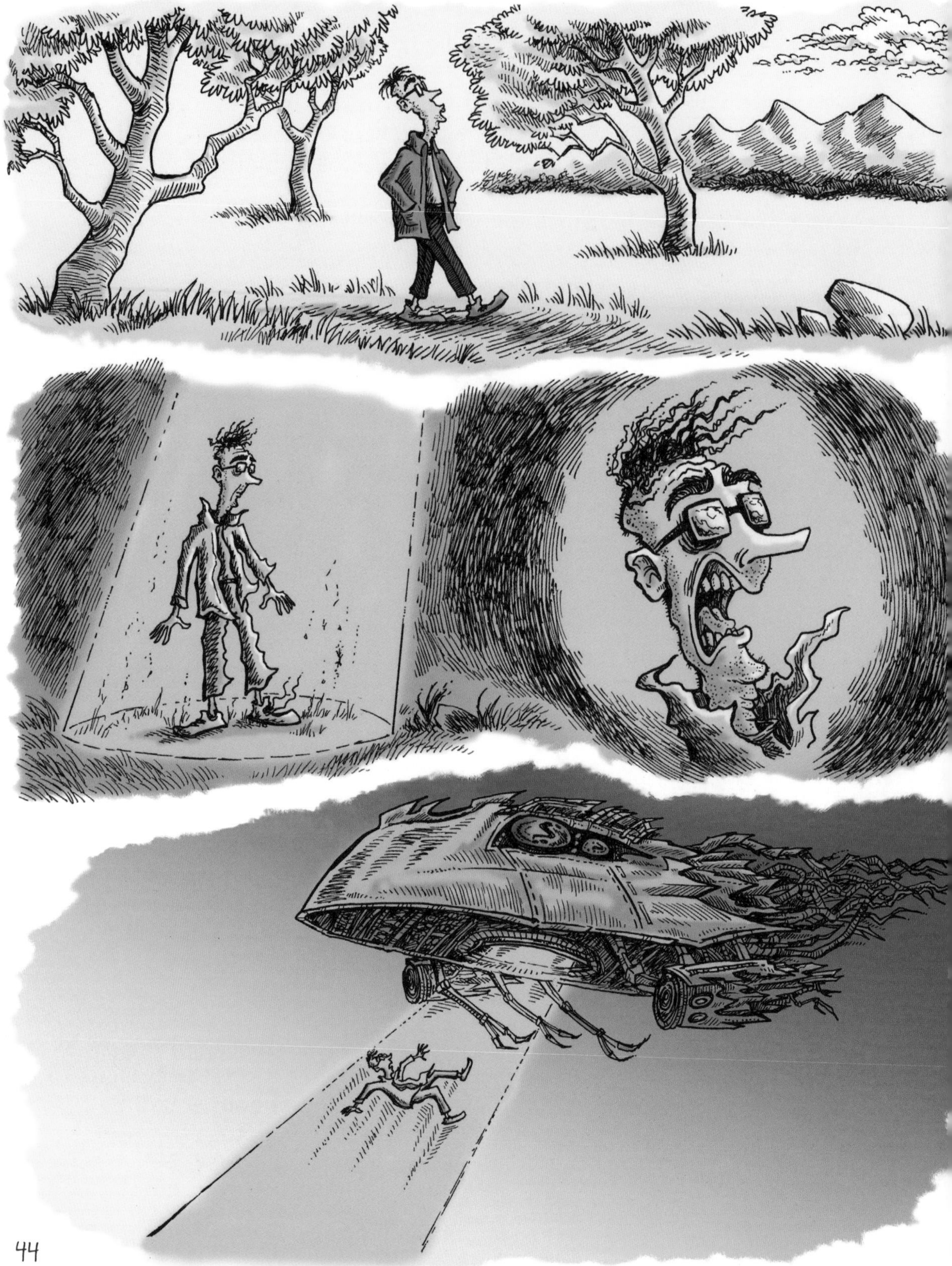

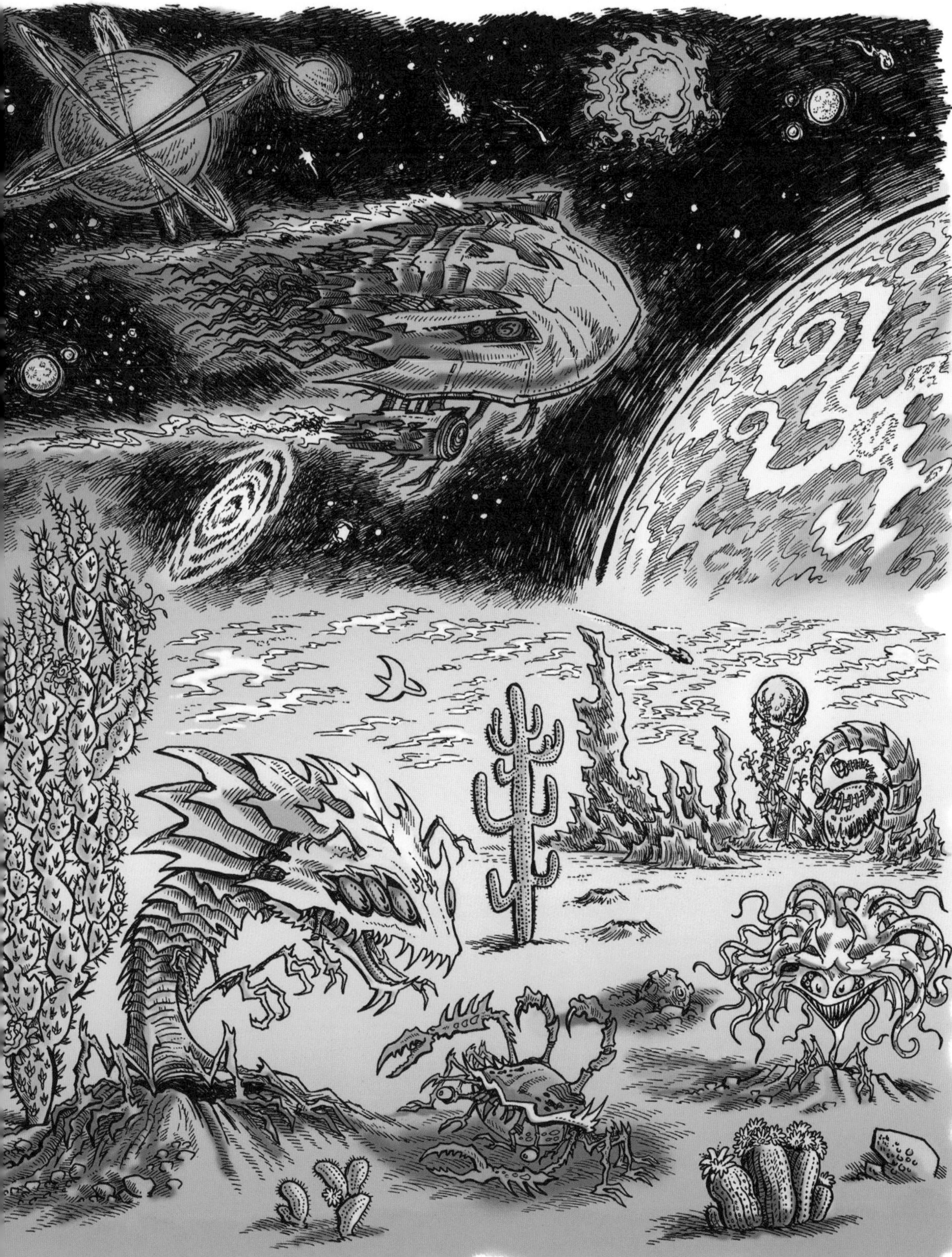

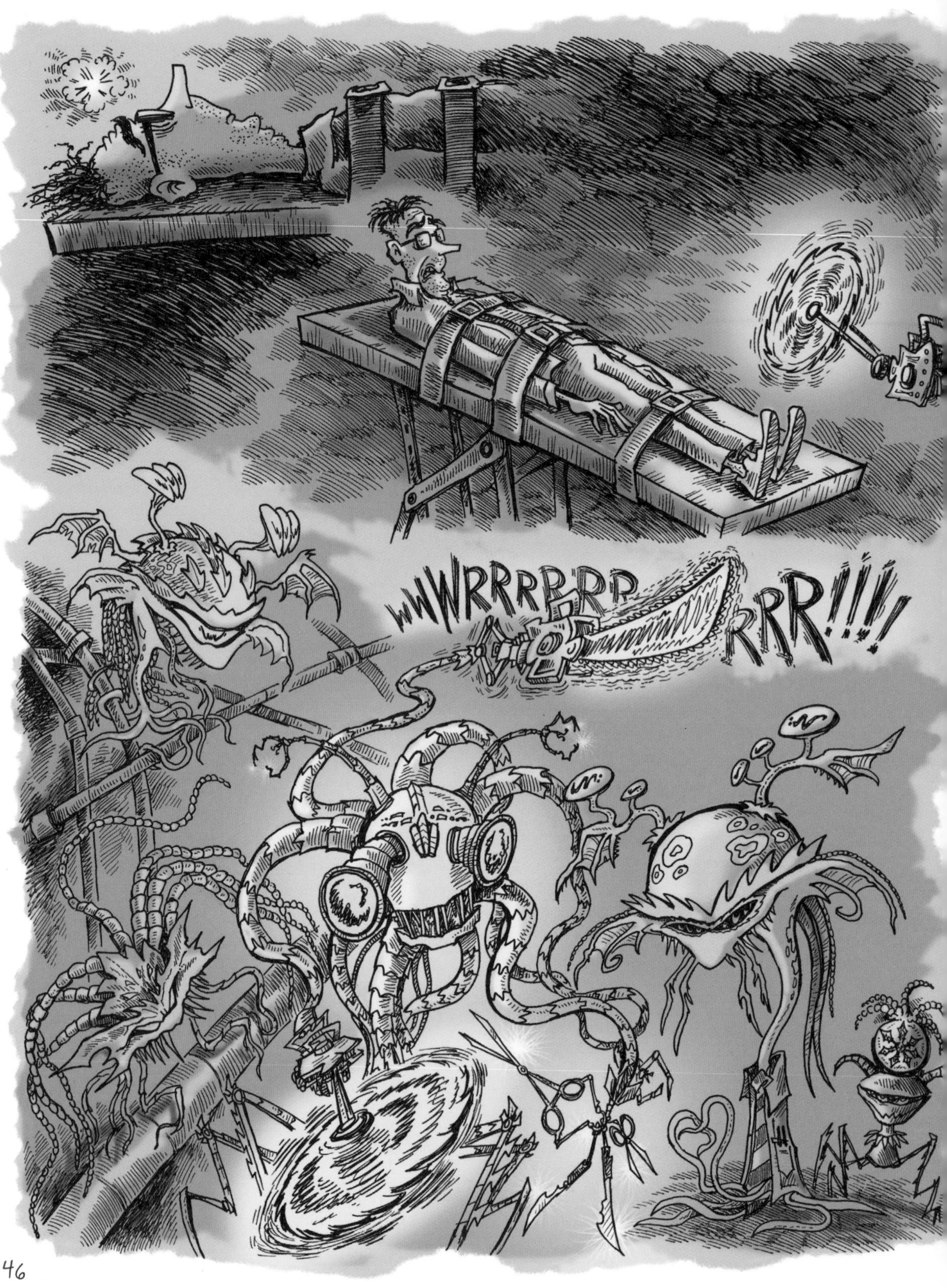
wwWRRRRRRRRRR!!!!

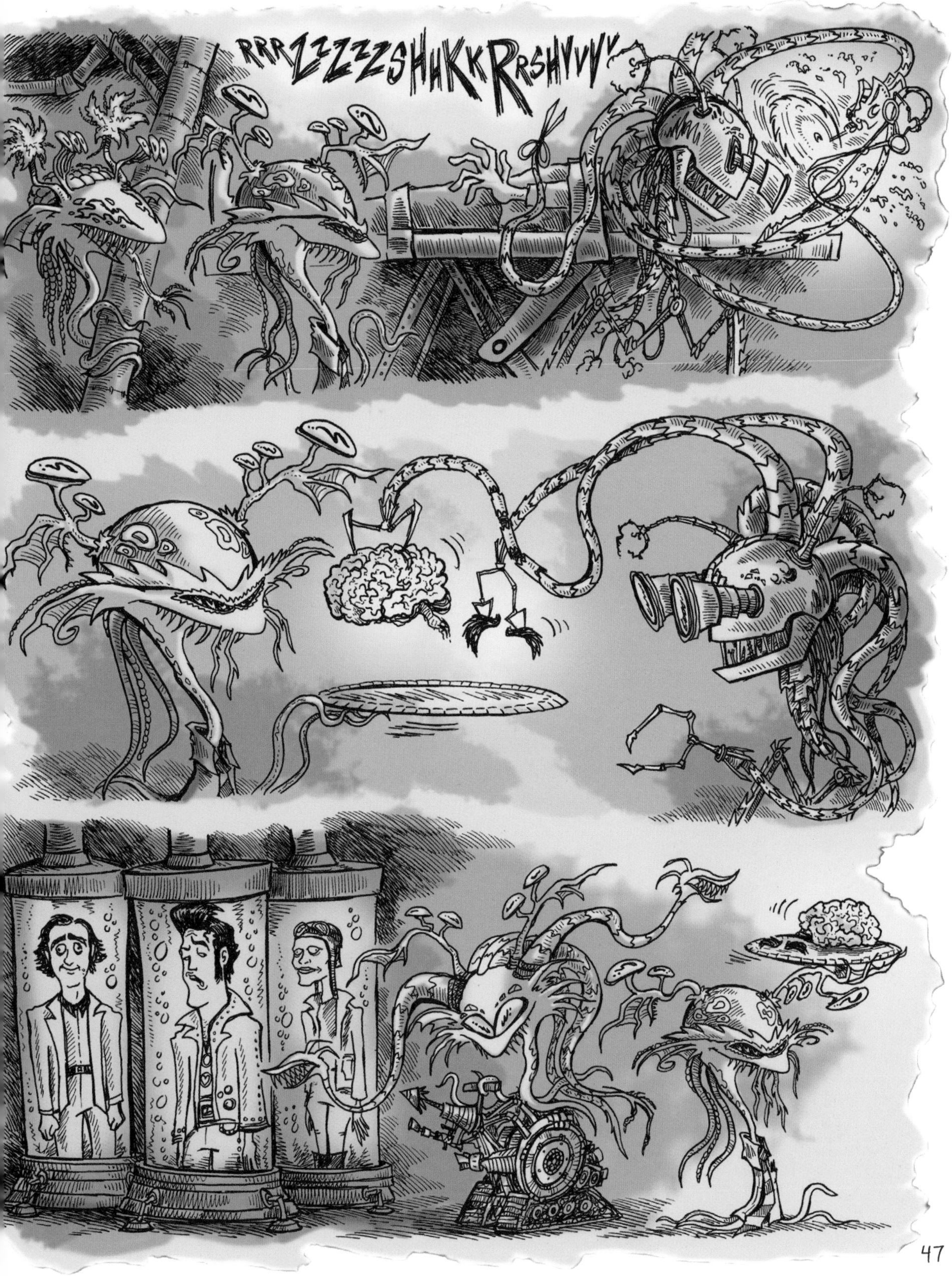
RRRZZZZZSHUKKRRSHVVVV!

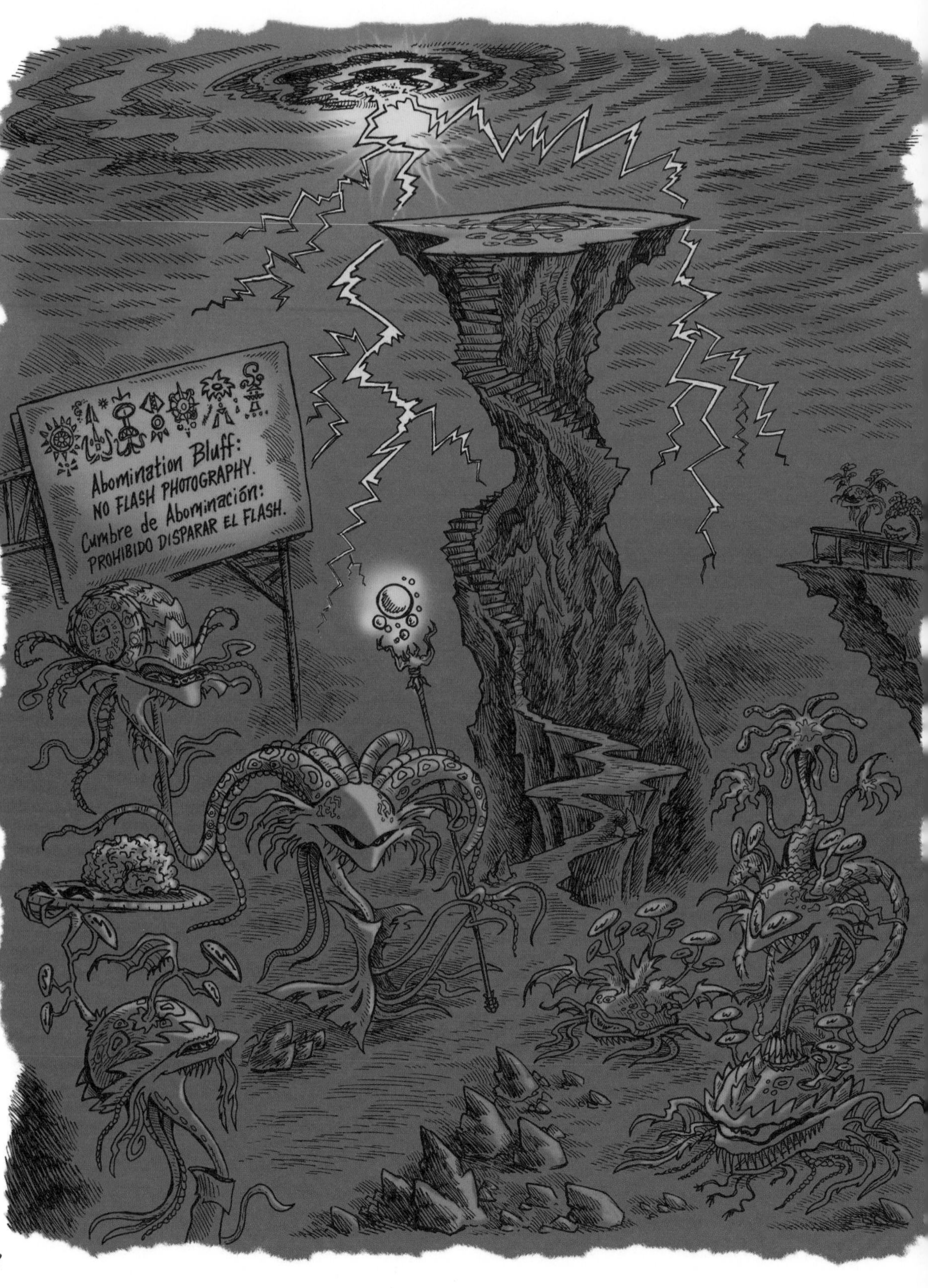
Abomination Bluff:
NO FLASH PHOTOGRAPHY.
Cumbre de Abominación:
PROHIBIDO DISPARAR EL FLASH.

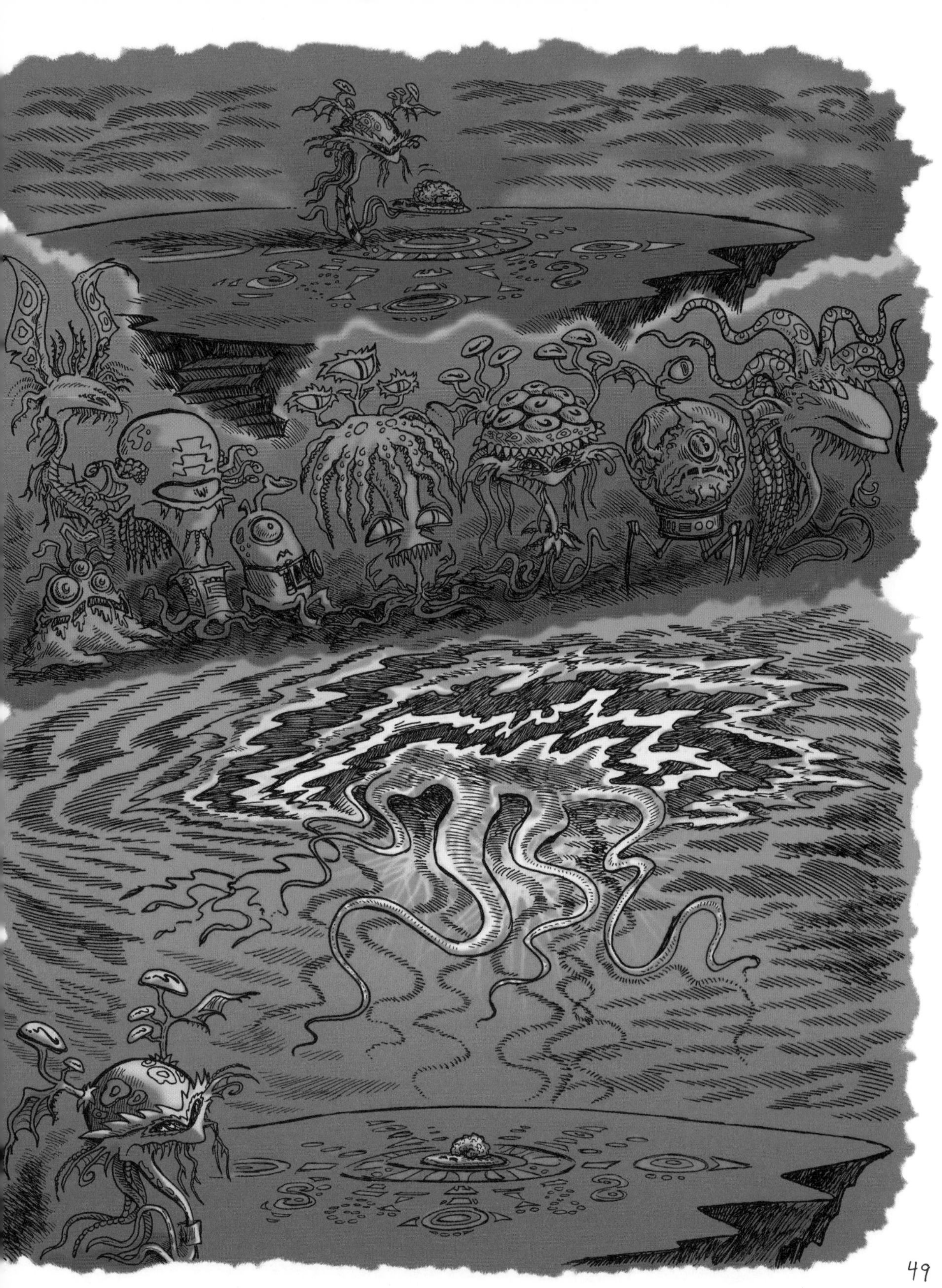

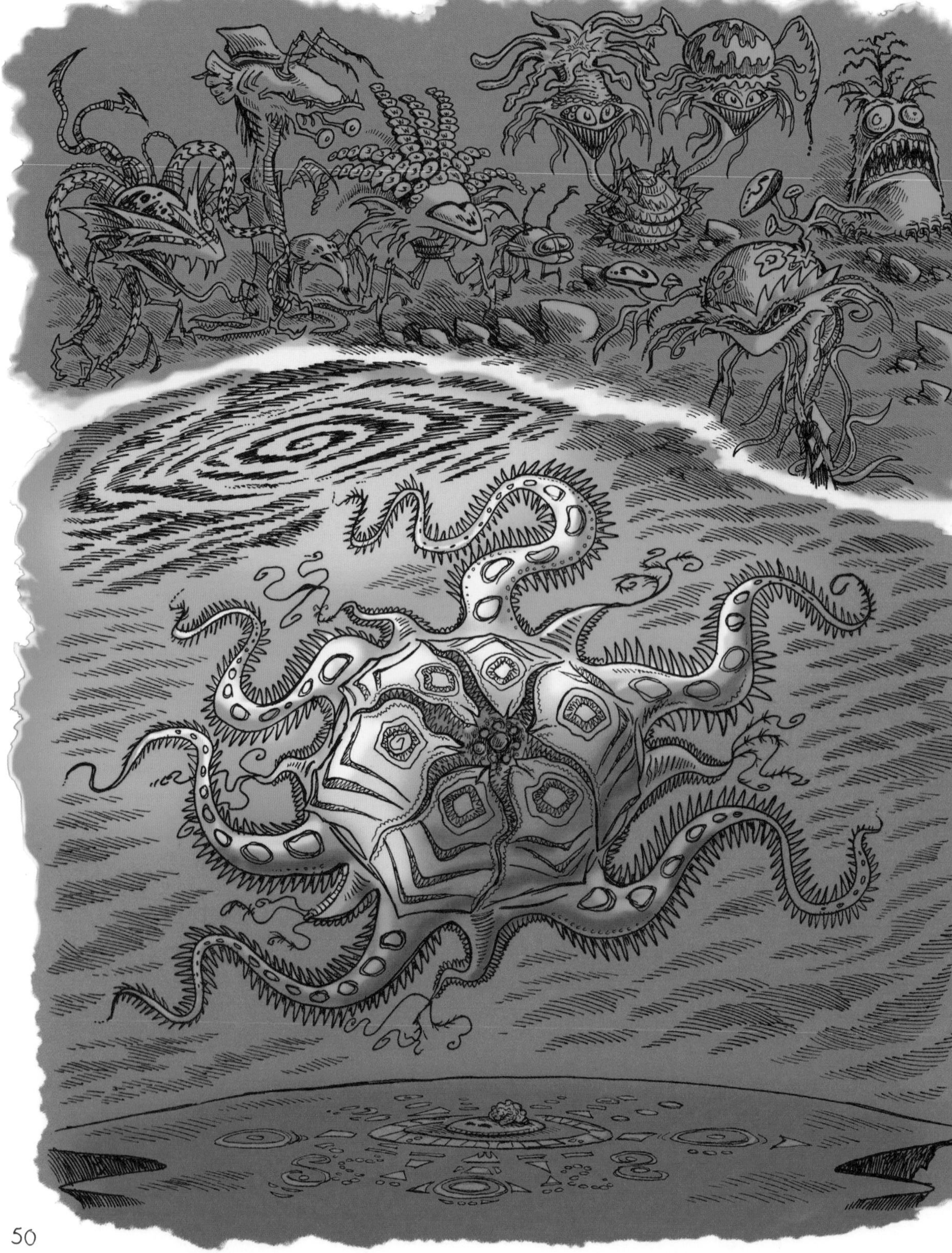

"Aw...What's an Eldritch Abomination Gotta do to get some steak sauce with its Human Sacrifices?"

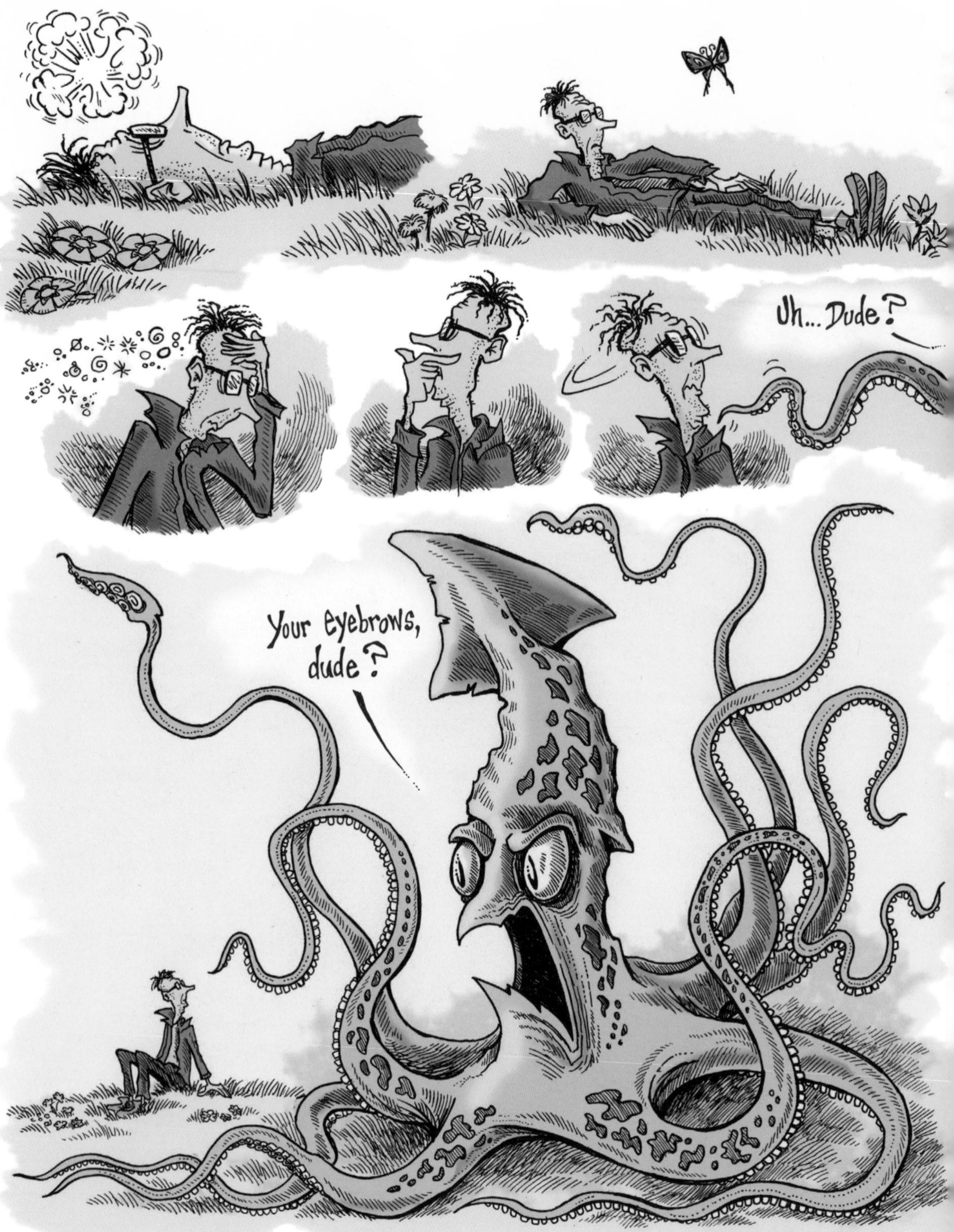
Uh... Dude?
Your eyebrows, dude?

The odd fellow folded his hands and leaned back.
His story (if it could be called a story) was done.

The old man removed his spectacles, cleaned them with his shirtsleeve, and returned them to their perch.

"<u>That</u>...is a story I won't bother discussing."

He pulled another room key from his pocket and slid it across the table.

"Second door on the left."

The odd fellow accepted the key, pushed in his chair, and drifted out of the kitchen.

The table suddenly seemed impossibly long—
a desolate wasteland stretching out over the horizon. The old man sat at the far end of this wasteland, chewing the tip of his pipe. Mr. York was now painfully aware of even the slightest sounds: the relentless ticking of the hall clock, the patting of rain on the window glass, the mousy rustling of the old lady in the next room.

Finally the old man removed the pipe from his mouth. "So," he said. His voice sounded deeper than before. *Amplified.* "Let's hear your story."

Mr. York licked his lips and ran a hand through his hair — which, he'd noted, was starting to recede. He was desperate to stall for even a few more seconds, but in the en it was useless. The old man's eyes were boring into him, and he had no story to tell.

"I... I'm sorry, sir, but I have no story to tell you." Mr. York tried to maintain eye contact with his host, but he felt his gaze slipping down to his hands, which were squirming below the table.

"What do you mean?" asked the old man. His voice was low and steady, like a carnivore preparing to ambush its prey.

"I mean I can't think of a single story worth telling. I've led a rather dull life, I suppose."

"*Balderpish!*" snapped the old man. "Surely you can think of something worth sharing! Those other three yo-yos managed. The first two told stories in <u>verse</u>, for crickity's sake!"

Mr. York's mind gave one last attempt to scrounge up a story... *a humorous anecdote, a whimsical fable, a fairy tale, a limerick... even a nursery rhyme might suffice!* ...But **nothing.** Mr. York could think of *nothing* to satisfy the old man.

"I'm sorry," Mr. York repeated. "I've never had any true adventures of my own, you see, and I've never given it much thought at that. Perhaps, if you'll give me a room, I'll think of a story as I sleep, or I could make one up overnight."

"Hogposh!" bellowed the old man. "The deal is this: *No Story, No Room!* And as long as I'm alive, that rule stays! Now make with a story, or get out of my house!"

And he punctuated his ultimatum by pounding his fist on the table.

The old lady appeared in the kitchen doorway, and Mr. York turned to her, hoping for sympathy. He found none. The kindness had left her eyes, and now they just looked beady. She shook her head and turned away.

"You know, I think you really <u>do</u> have a story to tell, but you just don't want to share it with a scraggly old man like me," growled the old man. "You think you're too good for me, don'tcha?"

"No!" Mr. York gasped. "That's not true!"

"Then tell your story or get <u>OUT</u>!"

Mr. York's jaw slumped open. He stared bug-eyed at the old man, unable to speak or think clearly. Finally he mustered enough sense to hobble from the kitchen, stumble out the front door, and trudge back into the gloom of the swamp.

The rain had softened to a misting, but the air was damp and seemed heavy in Mr. York's lungs as he walked the same trail he'd traveled only a short while earlier. The scene felt unreal, and more than once he wondered if he might actually be home in bed dreaming.

He wasn't.

Gradually his scattered wits returned to him, and with them came the pangs of panic.

There will be another house, he assured himself. *The Old Man and Old Lady couldn't be out here all alone. There will be others. Maybe a town. Keep your head and you'll get by. Perhaps you'll even laugh about all this tomorrow.*

But deep down Mr. York had his doubts, and with each passing minute he was more and more certain that he would never make it out of the swamp. He tried to recall the old lady's warning... *what had she said?*

Lacerating Manti? Shlutherglurks? Preposterous! She was crazy.

The old man, too. *Both* crazy.

Still, this logic was of little comfort.

He plodded along, giving little or no thought to the direction in which he was moving. Every now and then he'd scan the swamp for houselights. He saw none, and it seemed the swamp was growing denser.

A sudden rustling jerked him from his stupor. He whirled around, eyes bulging with fear.

"Who's there?!" he shouted. No answer. He peered into the shadows.

"Someone's there! I heard you! Show yourself, please!"

An excruciating pause, then a gravelly voice:

"Relax, Slim! Call off your hounds. It's only me..."

A short, hunched figure appeared in the path.
He was clad in a ratty jacket two sizes too
big and a beat-up porkpie hat. His hair
was unkempt, his beard scruffy, his
nose long and cucumberish. His eyebrows
were as untamed as luna moth antennae,
and below them a pair of yellow eyes
glowed like queasy stars.

The little fellow tipped his hat.

"No cause for alarm. It's just me,
Percival Trullus, at your soivice.
Now tells me, stringbean, what's
a soft fry like yourself doing out
at a brutal hour like dis in a
rotten place such as here?"

"My name is Jonathan York, and
I'm lost. Perhaps you know a way
out of this swamp?"

The little fellow grinned.
"Soitenly I does! I'm a
boney-fide regular 'round dese
parts, see. 'Coise, it would
take da better part of da night
to get out, and it's always risky
to travel after dark. Ya'd be
better off bunking down in a
safe house for a spell, Mr. Yoik."

59

"Then do you know a place I could spend the night?"

The little fellow's grin widened.
"Mayhaps I does, Mr. Yoik. 'Coise, being from outta town, I s'pect ya ain't up on proper swampland proy-tee-col, now is ya?"

Mr. York shrugged.

"I'm saying it's good and proper manners for an outsider to humor da locals wit' a token tip, 'specially when dey's asking favors."

"I'm sorry, Mr. Trullus, but I don't have any money."

The little fellow chuckled.
"Don't take dis da wrong way, Yoiky, but I tink I knows a liar when I hears one. Heh heh."

Mr. York turned his pockets inside out, spilling some lint, a frayed piece of dental floss, and an old bottle cap. The little fellow scooped up the bottle cap and polished it on his sleeve. He opened the side of his jacket, revealing an assortment of trinkets hanging from the lining.

"Better den nuttin', I s'pose," he muttered as he tucked the bottle cap into a pouch.

60

"All right, you have your *tip*," said Mr. York. "Please tell me where I might spend the night."

"Right! Right!" The little fellow's grin had grown so wide it threatened to sever the top of his head. " 'bout a quarta mile down da path and off to da left dere's an ol' Whisple tree. Amid da whisples you'll find a door wit' a brass knocker. Knock tree times fast and tree times slow."

"Three fast and three slow," Mr. York repeated.

"Ya got it! Do dat and you'll find your place to spend da night."

With that, the little fellow tipped his hat again and slipped back into the shadows.

Mr. York reset his pockets and moved on, hoping his instincts were wrong and C. Percival Trullus had told it true.

61

He'd only walked another ten minutes before he saw the whisple tree. It loomed high into the night sky, its limbs curling and twisting like the tentacles of some terrestrial cephalopod. He ran his hands along the tangled vines until they found a small wooden door with a brass knocker, just as the little fellow had described.

He clutched the knocker, paused at the shock of cold metal against his skin, and delivered three quick knocks, followed by three slow ones.

Silence.
He fidgeted, wondering if he had somehow done the knocks wrong. Just when he became convinced that he had been cheated out of a bottle cap, the ground opened beneath his feet. Before he had time to shout, scream, or even **eep**, poor Mr. York was plunged into darkness.

He landed with a thud in a dimly lit room. The walls were lined with an array of stolen goods: bags of coins, stashes of jewelry, fancy fur coats...
To the left was a rack of various knives, swords, and other weapons Mr. York could not name. Although his sheltered life had limited his knowledge of the world's shadier aspects, it was clear to him that he had blundered into the hideout of thieves.

The sting of an icy blade being pressed to the nape of his neck made him wince.

"'old still, stranger, less ye be wishin' t' see th' color of yer insides!"

They were the weirdest-looking thieves Mr. York had ever seen. Their features were hideous: one had a long, gar-like snoot, another had eight spidery limbs. They were dressed in a hodgepodge of ragged clothing, no doubt collected from past victims.

"'E's a sickly 'un, by th' looks of it," sneered the gar-faced thief. "All thin 'nd pale-like."

"Aye," agreed the eight-legged thief. "Likely won't be of much use, 'spects I."

A tall thief with an eel-like neck held a rusty blade to Mr. York's chin.

"On yer feet, wretch!"

Mr. York wobbled upright and put his hands in the air.

"Please! I didn't mean to trespass! I was only following directions given to me by—"

"Shut yer grub-hole!" hissed eel-neck.

"Empty yer pockets!"

Mr. York flipped his pockets inside out for a second time that night. A lone scrap of unraveled dental floss floated to the ground.

"Gracklefetters!" spat the eight-legger. "'e 'in't worth a tuppence! What is that id'jit Trullus thinkin' sending us these empty-pocketed weaklings?"

A tiny thief sporting an oversized helmet leaped forward and brandished a mace. "Mash 'im, sez I! Slice 'im t'ribbons 'nd use 'im as Niperlunge bait!"

The helmet-headed thief swung the mace mere centimeters from Mr. York's nose. The breath caught in Mr. York's chest. He expected his brains to be on the floor in a second or two.

"Stop!" called a voice from the back of the hideout. "Let down your weapons, fools, and step away from our guest!" It was a cold, throaty voice. A voice that sounded like water burbling through a sunless cavern.

The thieves lowered their blades and stepped aside. There stood a figure draped in a cloak and wide-brimmed hat. The shadows cast by the hat completely obscured the figure's face.

"What is your name, comrade ?" asked the figure.

Though still very afraid, Mr. York could feel his panic subsiding. It was replaced by a stifling coldness.

"J-J-Jonathan York!" he squeaked.

"Welcome to our 'umble 'ome, Mr. York. My name is Phintesmo Blyme, and together we are the West Bleekport Gang."

The cold needled Mr. York's spine
West Bleekport Gang?
Where had he heard that before

"You're shivering, Mr. York," said Blyme. He tilted his head up, and now Mr. York could see he was smiling. It was a broad smile, a smile full of gleaming dagger-teeth. "There's no need to be frightened. We're all friends here. Isn't that so?"

The other thieves bobbed their heads in agreement. "And now you're our friend too. Right, Mr. York?"

Blyme drew close enough for Mr. York to make out his face, and he was horrified to see it was *all* smile—no eyes, no nose... just a huge, dagger-toothed grin.

"S-sure," Mr. York stammered, nearly choking on his answer.

"Shake."

Mr. York reluctantly shook Blyme's gloved hand. It was firm and cold.

67

"Gooood. Now that we're friends, we'll let you in on our little project. Y'see, we're in the midst of a genuine treasure 'unt. Eh, comrades?"

The other thieves tittered.

"Y'll join our treasure 'unt, won't you, Mr. York?"

"Well, actually, I—"

"Sure ya will! Everyone likes a treasure 'unt! Now no sense in 'anging 'round the ol' 'ideout. There's work t' be done

Blyme turned and drifted up a flight of crude stairs. Mr. York, on the verge of a shock-induced torpor, was frozen in place until the gar-faced thief gave him a shove. His legs moved involuntarily, jerking up and down like the legs of a marionette, carrying him outside with the West Bleekport Gang.

68

They moved away from the trail and through the wilds of Halfrock.
They skirted sinkpits and murkholes, sidestepped boulders and brackpools,
passed trees twisting skyward like the limbs of long-dead insects
and brooks burbling bad poetry.

"D'ye 'ear that, Mr. York?" said Blyme.

Mr. York listened. Somewhere in the gloom he
heard voices singing... or *caterwauling*.

"Shivaree Sirens, Mr. York," said Blyme.
"Halfrock's banshees, we calls 'em. It's said they sing
it after the swamp claims a victim. Or before.
I can never remember which."

The voices crescendoed to an ear hair-singeing shriek,
then fell silent, and Mr. York could only hear the blood
thumping in his head.

"It's going t' be a good night, Mr. York,"
said Blyme.

At last they reached a dark pit of brackish water and algae.

"Being new to our organization, you shall 'ave the 'onors, Mr. York," said Blym

The other thieves pushed Mr. York forward.

"What do you mean? What are we doing here?"

"We need to retrieve the key to the treasure chest. Can't open a chest without a key, can we, Mr. York?"

"I suppose not. Where's this key?"

Blyme gestured to the pit.

"D-down _there_?!?" Mr. York squealed.

"Aye, but more specific'lly, it's in the belly of the Bogglemyre."

Mr. York felt faint.

"W-what's the Bogglemyre?"

70

"Biiiig monster," answered the gar-faced thief. "Big mouth. Big hunger. Eats all. Swallered one of our mates when 'e 'ad the key in 'is possession. Now the key's in its stomach."

"But how am I supposed to get the key out of this monster's belly?"

"Oh, there's a way," grinned Blyme. "Y'see, the Bogglemyre's got lots of teeth, 'e only uses them to keep 'is meals *in* after 'e swallers them whole. Once you're the Bogglemyre's belly, you should be able to get the key no problem."

"You mean I have to let this thing *EAT* me? You can't be serious!"

Mr. York could see they were.

"But... how do you expect me to get back _OUT_?!"

"That's the tricky part. See, the Bogglemyre's got an odd digestive system — what it don't use it spits back up as waste. Once you're in the beast's belly, you've only 'bout ten minutes 'fore its gut juices melt your flesh and turn your bones to clay. So if you wants t'make it out again with our key, you 'ave to do something that makes the Bogglemyre think you're not worth 'avin' in its gut pit so it'll spit you back up 'fore you've through digesting.

"Either way you're coming back up... as your whole self or as a pile of 'alf-digested scraps. Which d'yer prefer?"

"This is ridiculous!" cried Mr. York. "There has got to be a better way!"

The thieves drew their weapons in uniso[n]
Blyme stepped forward, fingering his jagged
blade and flaunting his cold, dagger-toothed smi[le]
"Now 'olds it there, Mr. York
You said you was game to our
treasure 'unt. Why, I seer
t' recall y' shakin' me o[n]
hand on it. Am I
right, Shmeevil?"

"Aye!" piped the gar-faced thief.

"T' what I thought," said Blyme.
"And 'round these parts that's
a binding agreement."

"Yes, but—" began Mr. York.

"We may be thieves, but we's
still good 'nd proper, 'in't we, Sleuth?"

"True," chimed the eel-necked thief.

"'Course it is!" hissed the advancing Blyme.

"Just let me—" whined Mr. York, stepping back.

"And being the proper gentlefolk we is, we don't much appreciate comrades going back on their word, 'specially when we go out of our way to let 'em in on our business."

"But if I could please just—"

Mr. York realized too late that the thieves had been backing him to the edge of the pit. Blyme leaned forward and tapped Mr. York on the chest, and poor Mr. York toppled into the inky water with a yelp.

Mr. York floundered to the surface and groped for the bank. The gar-faced thief shoved him back into the pit.

"Please!" Mr. York begged. "Don't do this!"

"Remember the plan," said Blyme. "Get the key and get out some'ow

"No! I can't do it! and I'm demanding you let me out NOW!

To his surprise, the thieves stopped grinning and backed away from the edge of the pool. For a split second he believed his outburst had startled them into submission.

The booming gurgle behind his back made him think otherwise

He had just enough time to glimpse the mass of tentacles and stalk eyes before its colossal mouth engulfed his body and swallowed him whole.

The horror of being eaten alive was too much for Mr. York, and his brain switched off for a minute or two. When he regained consciousness, he found himself in a slimy, pulsating chamber.

Where am I? he wondered. It didn't take him long to remember the ugly truth: he was in the Bogglemyre's belly.

He struggled to overcome his rising panic and think clearly. What was he supposed to do in here? He was expected to get something, wasn't he?

...a *Key!* Yes, he needed to find a key.

But... but why did that matter *now*? Why shouldn't he put all his effort into escaping with his *life*?

Because if you escape WITHOUT the key, the West Bleekport Gang will send ya right back in! warned his now-coherent brain.

His hands searched blindly in the surrounding slosh until they nudged something small and metal. His fingers probed the object... Yes, it *was* a key.

He clutched it in his left hand. Step one—*done*. Now the hard part: *getting back out.*

He extended his legs and kicked at the slippery walls around him. They stretched, but snapped back into place as soon as his feet pulled away. He kicked again, harder this time. Still no use. The Bogglemyre was built to handle prey much stronger than measly Mr. York.

He tried reaching up, hoping he might grab hold of the beast's tonsils and trigger a gag reflex. No luck; the Bogglemyre's gullet had constricted.

He took a deep, sobbing breath. The air was stale... *stifling*, and now he feared he might suffocate.

And how long did Blyme say he had before the creature's stomach acid did its work?

Now he could feel his own airway closing as anxiety set in, and his whole body started to tremble. He frantically clawed at the beast's stomach wall. Something wriggled — a gut parasite, most likely. He recoiled with a moan and surrendered to the panic attack.

Hic!

Mr. York's torso jolted. He was no stranger to anxiety-induced hiccups, but these were especially powerful.

Hic! Hic!
Hic!

Over the years he'd learned tricks for stalling the hiccups, but it all seemed so pointless now. He would be digested for sure, and in a few hours the Bogglemyre would spit up his grisly remains.

Hic... Hic... Hic.....
HRUPP!!!

Mr. York froze. Had that last hiccup really come from *him*? No, certainly n—

hHRYUP!!!

The belly chamber jostled violently, and Mr. York was flung into the elastic walls.

He struggled to right himself, only to be thrown by yet another ultra-hic.

HRRUPH!!

Somehow the jolting of Mr. York's own hiccups had triggered a massive hiccup attack in his consumer.

HRRUPT!

Mr. York's body was tossed back and forth like a grape in a bowl of Jell-o. An unsettling thought flickered through his mind

What's worse: *being liquefied alive by digestive ju* or *being rattled to a pulp by monstrous hiccups*?

Luckily, Mr. York was to suffer neither; the Bogglemyre decided a seemingly harmless snack had turned disagreeable, and it was time to jettison the irritant. And so, with one great phlegm-rattling belch, the monster emptied its stomach, and Mr. York was launched from the pit like a human loogie.

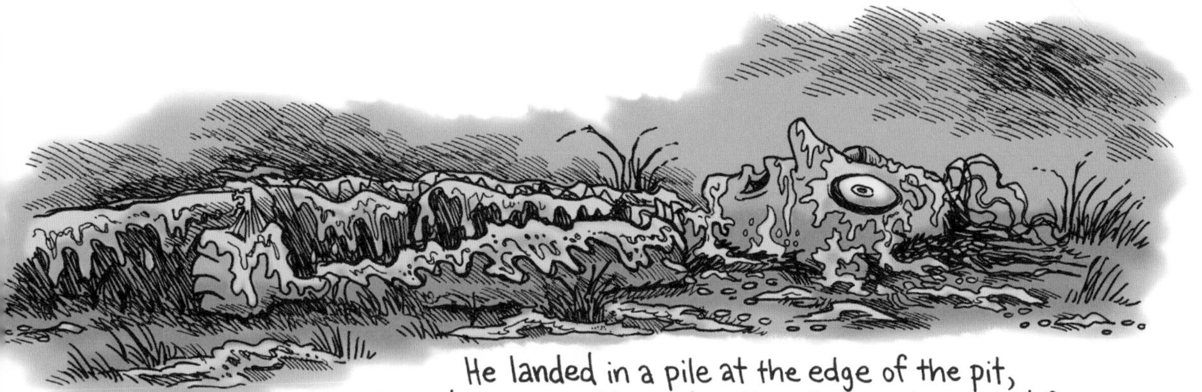

He landed in a pile at the edge of the pit, scarcely recognizable under the slime. He rasped for air and rolled onto his back, relishing fresh oxygen and a victory over improbable odds. Sadly, his relief was short-lived, for when he opened his eyes he found the grotesque faces of the West Bleekport Gang beaming down at him.

"Did you get the key?" said Blyme.

Mr. York unclamped the fingers of his left hand, and the key fell to the ground. He'd been squeezing it so hard it had left a perfect imprint in his palm.

"Goood," Blyme cooed. "I must say we 'ad some doubts regarding your—shall we say—*abilities*, Mr. York. Mayhaps we've underestimated you."

The eight-legger snatched the key while the eel-necked thief hauled Mr. York to his feet.

"Now that I've got you your key, I'd like you to do me a favor... *please*," said Mr. York between coughs.

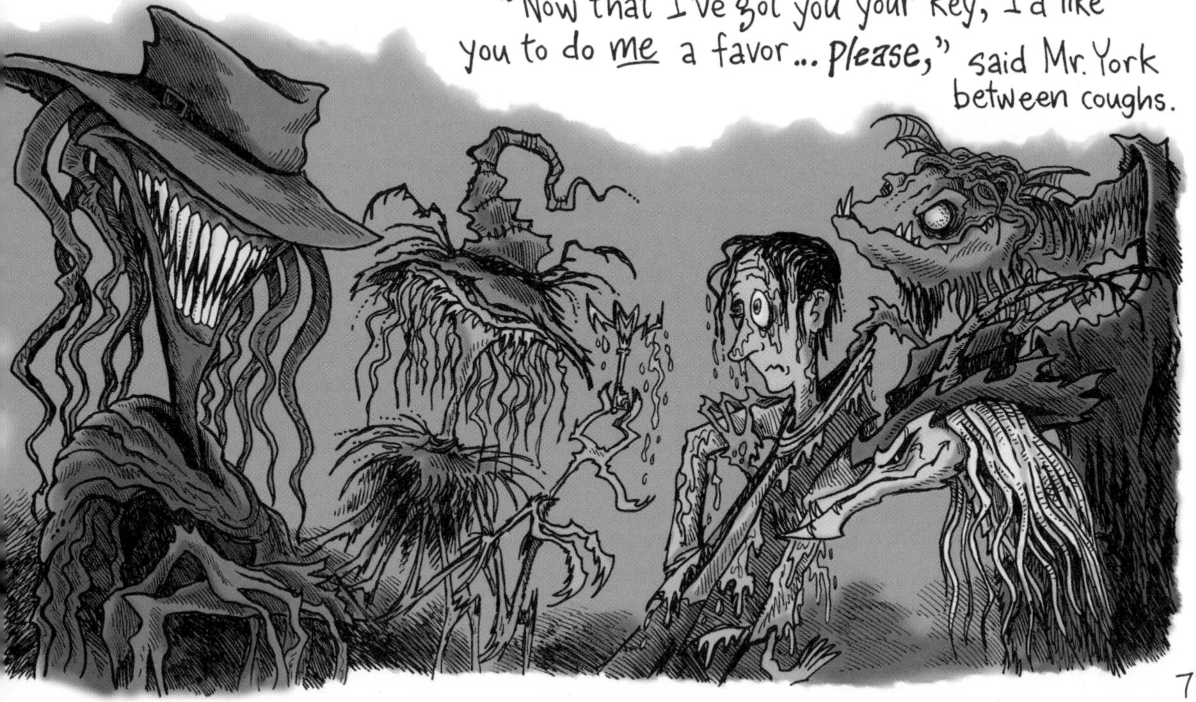

Blyme turned to Mr. York, his dagger-toothed smile unfaltering.

"Anything, dear friend."

"I want you to show me a place where I can spend the night, so in the morning I may leave the swamp and go home."

Blyme uttered a low, burbling chuckle. "O'course, Mr. York, o'course. But now we's in the midst of a treasure 'unt, and cutting a treasure 'unt down in its prime is 'ardly proper protocol. Am I right, Skabcraw?"

"Oyez 'ndeed!" snickered the eight-legger.

"Aye!" said Blyme. "Now come along, comrades. The game is nigh."

Mr. York resisted the urge to object. He figured the worst was over, and he preferred to stay on Blyme's good side, assuming such a thing existed.

The canopy waned and retreated, and trees were replaced by stretches of ne-like reeds. A mist surrounded the treasure hunters, wrapping them in its drils, turning the world white. The swamp had dissolved into a marshland.

Blyme stopped and pointed out at the motionless water.
"Out there."

Mr. York felt a chill skitter down his spine. "What's out there?"

"Our treasure, 'course. The one we're 'unting for. The one that was stolen from us."

"W-who stole it?"

Blyme ignored the question. "Now, to get our treasure back, we needs someone cross the marsh, and since our friend Mr. York 'andled the Bogglemyre commendably, I feels obliged t' nominate 'im for the job."

"Wait—wha—*what*?" said Mr. York.

The eel-necked thief raised his blade. "I'll second that!"

"I'll third!" hollered Helmet-head.

"All in favor of sending our dear Mr. York 'cross the marsh says 'Aye!'"

"Aye!" cheered the thieves in unison.

"All opposed?"

Mr. York raised a meek hand.

"Five against one. Ya float, Mr. York."

"Now hold on a minute!" stammered Mr. York. "I got the key back, didn't I? Doesn't that mean someone else should take a turn doing the dirty work?"

"Y' might believe so," grinned Blyme, "but it'd be a shame to pull a winner likens yourself to an 'alt when you're on such a winning streak."

Mr. York tried to argue, but the glitter of Blyme's blade in the mist ended further debate.
"What is it you want me to do?"

"In the middle of the water is a rocky island. The safest way t' get there is t' float y'self 'cross on something sturdy and buoyant."

"You mean on a boat?" interrupted Mr. York. "But we don't _have_ a boat."

The gar-faced thief pulled back a clump of reeds to reveal a large wooden barrel turned on its side. "No boat, but this'll do nicely."

"So," continued Blyme, "after floating on barrel t' the island, you'll find a cave. In the cave is a chest with our gang's insignia on it, same as the key. Bring it back to us, and we'll show you out of the swamp to a safe 'ouse."

"What lives in the cave?" Mr. York asked.

Blyme's grin widened. "The Terrakingpin."

"And what's that?"

"Never y'mind. With a bit o' luck, it'll be out hunting. If not, 'twas a pleasure doing business with you, Mr. York."

Mr. York wiped dried slime from his brow. "Very well. But this is the last favor I do for you thieves."

He bent and lifted the barrel, but Blyme snagged his wrist before he could cast off. "'old yourself, Mr. York. There's one more thing. We didn't tell you about the Fear 'im Gnott."

Mr. York licked his lips. "What's the Fear 'im Gnott? Not _another_ monster, I hope!"

"The Fear 'im Gnott dwells in the deeper parts of the marsh. It's not as big as the Bogglemyre, but just as 'ungry. Lucky for you it's deaf and blind."

"Then why should I fear it?"

"Y' shouldn't. You're in danger if you do. It can _sense_ your fear."

83

"I... I don't understand."

"Then listen close: the trick t' getting past the Fear 'im Gnott is *NOT* to be afeared. That's where the name 'Fear 'im Gnott' comes from. If you *do* show fear it'll seek you out and swaller you up quicker than the twitch of a weevil's feelers."

"But I can't force myself to be unafraid" sputtered Mr. York.

"Then you'd best learn fast. Tr' thinking 'appy thoughts, like you do when you 'uff pixie dust."

Mr. York stalled a moment and loo pleadingly into the faces of the West Bleekport Gang. He saw no hints of sympathy. He took a hea breath, lifted the barrel with "*Dang-the-Torpedoes*" haste, and cast off. He clung to the dry side the barrel, praying it would not flip and dunk him.

The thieves faded into the mist, and Mr. York found himself alone in a sightless, soundless world. Occasionally a reed would brush against the barrel's underside, and his heart would race. He squeezed his eyes shut and tried to ignore what might be lurking beneath the surface.

Happy thoughts, his brain reminded him. *Happy thoughts...Pink sunrises...
...The sound of summer leaves in the breeze... Baby otters playing in the river...*

Something slithered alongside the barrel. The movement was slight,
but this time Mr. York felt certain it was not just a reed.

Happy thoughts! his brain squealed. *Orange sunsets...Fall apples...uh...
Apple pie...at...at Thanksgiving!*

Ripples appeared to the left of the barrel. Seconds later they surfaced
on the right. The thing, whatever it was, was circling him.

The voice in his head was now a shriek: *The song of Cicadas in late spring...* *Clear starry nights... PUNCHING MR. JONESMITH SMACK-DAB IN HIS UGLY PUG-NOSE!*

Mr. Jonesmith had been Mr. York's manager at the Brockleport General Store for the last three years. He w the sort of supervisor who might make you reorganize cereal aisle one week and then *re*-reorganize it back what it originally was the next. Being of the mildest temperament, Mr. York had followed his lead without question... but *NOW*, strangely, the thought of belting his employer square in the sniffer was quite satisfying the happiest thought he'd had all night, actually.

The ripples seemed to be slowing, so Mr. York ran the scene through his mind in detail:

He'd walk into the general store, and th would be Mr. Jonesmith behind his desk in the b office, photos of his freckly sons in Little Leag attire on the wall. And Mr. York would march u and— but *WAIT! THIS* isn't meek, stutterin Mr. York! Ho Ho *NO! THIS* is slick, suave Mr. York, with arched eyebrows like... *like... SEAN CONNERY!* And he would wind up and *WHOOOSH—POP* Ol' Jonesy-Smitty right in th puss (which looked like something Dr. Seuss might've doodled on an off-day). And then Mr. York would snap his fingers and say—

—GerrRtch!

The barrel scraped against the shore of the island. Mr. York snapped out of his happy place and glanced over his shoulder. The water was flawless; not a ripple in sight. He'd made it past the Fear 'im Gnott.

He crept onto solid ground and strained his eyes into the mist. A dark mass loomed before him, and as he inched closer he saw the cave's mouth.

He tossed a pebble inside and heard it plink off another stone. He waited...

...*Silence*. No roars or bellows or *Fee-Fi-Foes*.

He tugged the hem of his vest and wished he had a collar to pop—the Mr. York of his fantasy wore his collar popped.

"Here goes nothin',"
he whispered.

He *hoped* it was nothin'.

It didn't take long to find the treasure chest. It was small and carelessly stashed behind a pile of yellowed bones. He scooped it up, tucked it under his arm, and turned to leave.

And then the ground shook.

Footsteps. Like the footsteps in a dinosaur movie. Like the footsteps you hear just before an expendable character gets chomped.

He froze mid-step, hoping, *praying* he wasn't an expendable character.

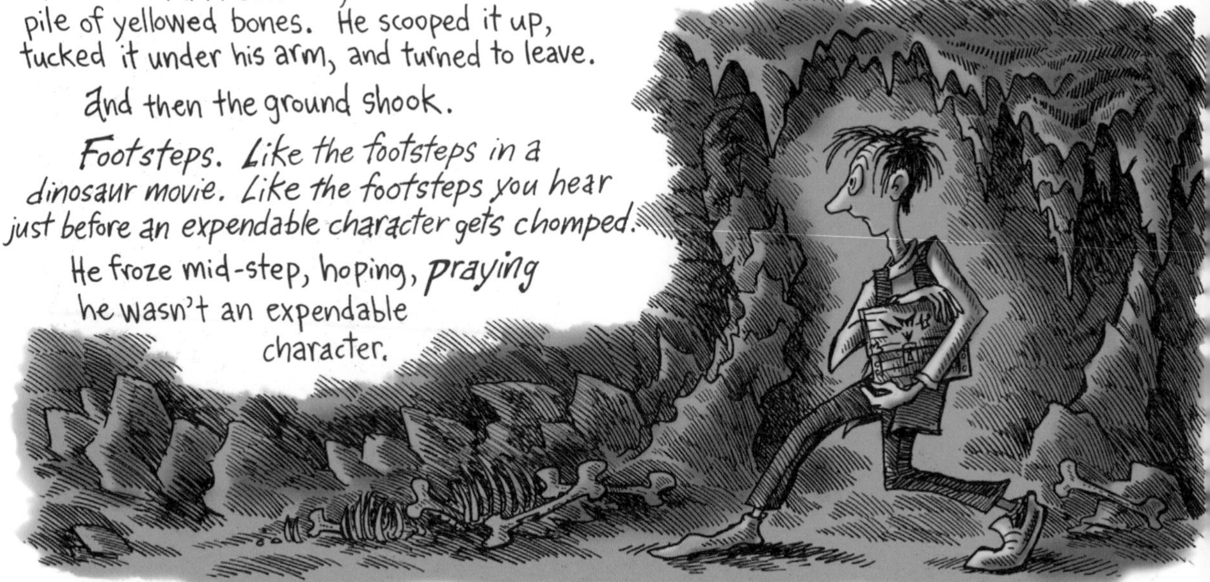

And then the cave's mouth was filled with a *tremendous* repti Mr. York had seen snappers before, heard tell of whoppers that could lop off fingers, but ***this*** put even the fishiest bait shop rumors to shame. It was... *GiGUNDA*, as they'd say in Brockleport. Its armor twisted into gnarled plates and spikes. Its neck, fully extended, was long and serper yet thick as an old tree trunk. Its head was dominated by terribl snapping jaws.

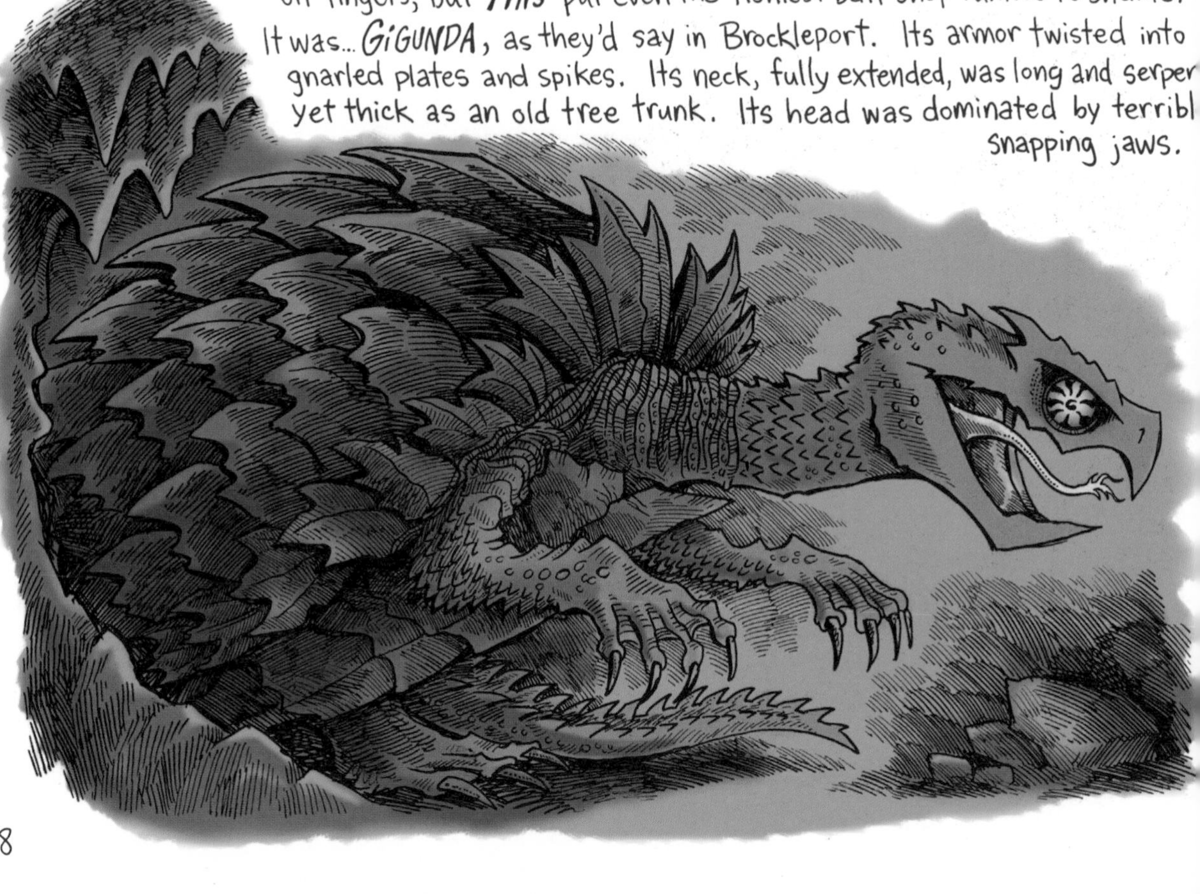

The snapper clapped its beak.

"*And what do I detect?*" it said in a surprisingly elegant voice.
"*A trespasser, I suspect!
A thief, quite probable, I deduce.
Speak, wretch! Your name and purpose, I demand!*"

"My name is Jonathan York. Please, I mean you no harm,
O Mighty Terrakingpin." Mr. York was stunned by the
clarity of his own voice.

"*Ha! Miserable stooge! You can only wish the Terrakingpin was here in
my stead; were that the case, your life might be salvaged. But alas,
he has been gone several nights, foraging on the far western side of the
swamp. I am his mate, the TerraQUEENpin, and if your bony legs
fail to quake at the mere mention of my name, you must be mad!*"

Mr. York smiled politely and gave a little bow. He figured his minutes were numbered,
t the Terraking-er—queenpin seemed to enjoy hearing itself speak.

"Though I am very afraid, Your Majesty Terraqueenpin, I am also awed. I've traveled far and wide, yet never have I seen such an impressive specimen."

The Terraqueenpin opened its beak again and leaned close enough for Mr. York to see the pale yellow lining of its throat. Its limited facial muscles made its emotions hard to read, but Mr. York could sense it was pleased.

"And I should not have expected you to! I am the pinnacle of power! The apex of awe! My armor: impenetrable! My jaws: devastational! Fear and admire me at once, puny mortal!"

Mr. York bobbed his head. "Oh, I do! I cannot even imagine a beast more phenomenal... except, perhaps, a dragon."

The Terraqueenpin hissed. "Dragons?! Bah! Worms! I am vastly superior to the most formidable dragon, I assure you. My armor is greater."

"Indeed!" agreed Mr. York. "Although it's worth noting that some dragons have wings."

"A trifle! I have no use for wings. They are flimsy and cumbersome. I favor swimming over flight."

"As do I! But I've also heard that most dragons breathe fire."

"And, pray tell, what use is this fire-breath you speak of?"

"Well, it's said that dragon fire is the most fantastic weapon on the planet. One exhalation can reduce an entire army to crispy bacon."

The Terraqueenpin's beak clamped shut. Finally it spoke again:

"In that case, I can breathe fire as well!"

"Ah! I thought you might! I suppose a magnificent [mo]nster like you would be expected to know the secret of fire-breath."

"Affirmatively! However, in compliance with the Oath of Fire-Breathers, I am sworn to secrecy. Therefore, you must prove to me that you know the secret of fire-breath before we continue this dialogue."

It just so happens I do know the secret," said Mr. York.

The Terraqueenpin's neck stretched forward.

"Then speak it, wretch!"

91

Mr. York cupped a hand to his mouth. "The secret of fire-breath is..."
He stalled as his mind grappled for a solution. "...big rocks," he said at last.

The Terraqueenpin nodded. "Ah...But what does one do with the big rocks? Prove to me that you know this."

"Why, you swallow them, of course! Once they are in your belly, your stomach acid melts them down to the magma they were made from, and your breath will turn to fire as a result."

The Terraqueenpin's eyes sparkled. "Indubitably!"

"Now, since you already knew this secret, why not treat me to a fire-breathing display? Consider it my last request before you eat me."

The Terraqueenpin fidgeted. "Oh... of course...I... I would, however, I've recently run out of belly magma, and I fear I shall need to refuel."

Mr. York shrugged. "No worries. There are plenty of boulders around."
He pointed to an especially hefty one near the back of the cave. "That should do the trick. Swallow it down, wait ten minutes, and leave me dazzled.
...Unless you lack the fire-breath talent, which, of course, would make you inferior to dragons."

"*Inferior? Me?!*" seethed the Terraqueenpin. "*Preposterous! Slanderous! You want fire, miserable peon? I'll show you fire!*"

The Terraqueenpin lunged at the boulder, opened its jaws to their fullest extent, and attempted to swallow the big rock whole. But boulders are seldom swallowed so easily, not even y reptilian monsters, and it took some creative maneuvering and an awful lot of croaking to squeeze the full quarry into its gullet.

The boulder lodged partway down, and the Terraqueenpin started to choke. After a minute of gagging and a few more of hacking it managed to vomit the boulder back up, and then, rasping for breath, it turned to snap Mr. York's head off, lest he spread word that the *Mighty Terraqueenpin*, scourge of Halfrock Swamp, was inferior to even the puniest dragon.

Of course, by this time Mr. York was already halfway across the marsh, the chest tucked snugly under his arm as he paddled the barrel to shore.

His heart thumped wildly. The hairs on the back of his neck stood on end, and his spi... prickled. But *this* time he was not suffering the symptoms of a panic attack. No, what h... felt was *exhilaration*. His victory over the Terraqueenpin had left him with a sense of excitement he had not experienced since early childhood. He was no longer plain ol' stuttering Mr. York—the man who, just a few hours ago, was thrown into a tizzy when he could not think of a story to tell. He was different now. He was a bold adventurer. He was a rugged explorer, the sort of character Robert Louis Stevenson would write about. He *was* the Mr. York of his fantasy, and he was a force
to be reckoned with.

The feeling was so intoxicating he almost forgot to fear the Fear 'im Gnott, and by the time he did remember he had safely crossed to the shallows of the other side, where the West Bleekport Gang was waiting for him.

Eel-neck and Gar-face pulled him from the barrel as Helmet-head snatched the chest from s arms. The eight-legger stabbed the key into the lock and popped the lid, revealing an sortment of coins, rubies, and zirconia necklaces. Blyme fingered the loot.

"Impressive," he grinned. "It's not often one encounters the BoggleMyre, the Fear 'im Gnott, a Terrakingpin in a single night and lives t' tell about it."

"I sez we sends 'im t' the Heckbender," cackled the helmet-headed thief.
"Then we'll see 'ow 'is luck 'olds out."

Mr. York could feel his newfound courage evaporating.
"Please! You promised you'd show me to a safe place to spend the night!"

Blyme nodded. "Aye. A bargain's a bargain. Don't listen to Grulmet, 'e's just ribbing you. We's honorable types, and we intend to keep our promise.

Now... follow me."

95

The rain had stopped and clouds had retreated, and above countless stars and planets winked in the infinite black. For the first time in many years, Mr. York felt a sense of awe as gazed into the night sky. He yearned to stay and let his mind get lost in the universe, but the gar-faced thief's blade was behind him, hovering like a wasp, eager to jab him back to reality should he linger.

"Where are we going?" he asked after some time.

"Northeast," said Blyme.

Mr. York felt a chill. Northeast? He vaguely recalled the old lady at the Cankerbury saying something about unspeakable horror at the swamp's northeastern edge.

"What's at the—"

Blyme's head twisted around, cutting Mr. York off mid-sentence.

"You'll see when we get there."

The canopy was thinning again, and soon the trees were skeletons, bleached and barkless, looming up from the swamp like wraiths. The mist reappeared, though now it was dry and icy, far from the humid, smothering fog of the marsh.

At last they stopped. Mr. York could faintly make out a large stone structure in the distance.

"The Keep of Sym-Iy-Kro," whispered Blyme.

The keep was old and lichen-encrusted. Blyme seized an iron doorknocker and knocked three times fast and three times slow. His knocks were answered by a reedy voice.

"'O goes thar?"

"Phintesmo Blyme and the West Bleekport Gang. We wish to make your master an offering

The hinges groaned as the doors swung open. A misshapen thing draped in rags shambled o

"Come in, West Bleekport Gang and guest. We bid welcome."

They made their way through a winding passage and up a spiral staircase. Mr. York
shoved his hands into his pockets, clenched his fists to keep them from trembling, and
tried to ignore the phantom shadows flickering on the walls around him. The stones had
assumed a greenish glow — some sort of luminous bacteria, perhaps.

They reached the top of the stairs and entered a circular room. Unearthly ornaments
sprawled across the floor, and in the room's center stood an altar.

"Many salutations," said a voice from a darkened corner.
"How good it is to have you in the court of Sym~Iy~Kro."

Blyme sheathed his blade.

"We come to you tonight with an offering of the 'ighest sort."

Something moved in the corner. Mr. York strained his eyes and thought he could see a spidery thing crouched in the shadows.

"How nice, I do declare! I sooo enjoy my offerings, Mr. Blyme. Please, do not hesitate to show me what you brought!"

The voice was rich and cheerful. In a different context, Mr. York might have associated it with a big, jolly man, the sort of grandfatherly figure one would expect to find carving the holiday turkey.

Blyme clapped Mr. York on the back. "This is Mr. Jonathan York. 'E might look a mite scrawny and sickly, but don't let 'is appearance fool you. 'e's as able-bodied as any of your servants. Mayhaps moreso."

"Is that true?"

The thing detached itself from the shadows and took form.

It stood very tall—eight feet, maybe more. Its body was skeletal, mounted on a pair of
ick legs, and its arms, even longer than the legs, called to mind something living under
basement floorboard. It wore a tattered cloak and a mask (*presumably* a mask)
ade from the skull of some extinct meat-eating animal, and above the
ask perched a hat that split into three ends. From a tear at the hat's rim peered a
air of burning orange eye sockets.

"Mr. York, Mistah Yawk!"

crowed the creature in a
using Southern preacher voice.

"How pleased I am to shake your hand!"

One of the creature's limbs shot across the room
nd seized Mr. York's hand, shaking him with such
vigor that poor Mr. York's whole body bobbled.
The grip was cold; Blyme's handshake seemed
balmy by comparison.

"See?" said Blyme. "I knew you two would 'it it off. 'Course, there is the matter of proper protocol."

The creature leaned back and bellowed laughter. "*Oh, mercy! Where are my manners!*"

He reached into his cloak and tossed Blyme a small leather bag.

Mr. York turned to the thieves, his face a caricature of desperation. "You're <u>selling</u> me to this demon⁇! After all I did for you⁇ Why, you're just a pack of slimy, double-crossing... *Bad Guys!*"

Blyme threw up his arms defensively. "What business is *this*, dear Mr. York? Calling us 'urtful names after we does you the biggest favor of your life? My, my! You came to us looking for shelter, and that's what we've given you! You'll be safe from rain and thieves and swamply beasties, and not only do you get a permanent 'ome, but a promising career as well — working with Sym-Iy-Kro, one of the most respected necromancers in all the world! If nothing else, you owe us a thankee kindly!"

With that, Blyme spun around and drifted back down the stairs, and Mr. York was left alone with Sym-Iy-Kro.

Mr. York tried to hide the fear in his voice.

"What are you going to do to me? Drink my blood?"

Sym-Iy-Kro clapped his hands and laughed again. "Oh, heavens, Mr. York, you slay me! 'Course I'm not going to drink your blood! We're partners now! You're part of the Sym-Iy-Kro family!"

"You mean you're making me your slave?"

Sym-Iy-Kro stopped laughing. "If you want it put in harsher words."

Mr. York crossed his arms. "And what if I refuse to serve you?"

"Ooo... You will. Like all the others, you will. They come in dragging their heels and cussing up a cyclone, but all that changes after they've been zombified."

"Zombified?!"

"Yes indeed! And once you've been zombified, all those anxieties and nasty feelings will wash away like snow in a springtime shower."

Mr. York had spent his life avoiding the unpleasant, yet he knew what a zombie was — a mindless, soulless minion to evil.

"Well, maybe I don't _want_ to be zombified."

Sym-Iy-Kro's voice became soft and gentle—the voice of a parent reassuring an upset chil

"Now, Mr. York, let's think this through, for truly this _is_ a big decision... You're a mild fellow, am I right? ...Yes, of course you are. You're not the sort of person who's cut out for his own adventures. No, you dread that sort of thing. And you dread risk. Risk is bad for routine."

Mr. York fidgeted.

"So why worry about that whole mess? Your emotions, your free will... they only complicate an otherwise safe and secure existence. Shed them. Surrender them to me, and I'll make all the hard decisions for you. You'll never have to fear getting lost in a swamp again. Doesn't that sound appealing?"

Mr. York shrugged. He felt numb.

"I thought it might. Now come..."

Sym-Iy-Kro led Mr. York to the altar and handed him a goblet filled with bubbling broth.

"One sip, that's all. One sip and all your uncertainty and anxiety will disappear, and this nightmare will be over."

Mr. York brought the goblet to his lips. He froze.

"What are you waiting for? Go on."

The goblet teetered in his hand... and then he lowered it. He looked SYM-Iy-Kro
ectly in his burning orange eye sockets.

"I'm sorry, but I can't let myself be zombified."

"What do you mean? What about your anxiety? Your fear of the unknown?"
M-Iy-Kro's voice had dropped to a whisper. *"One sip will eliminate those forever."*

"Yes, that might be nice, but I'd also lose my freedom."

*"Freedom is overrated. With freedom comes uncertainty. You hate uncertainty.
You hate adventures. Adventures are bad."*

"Maybe. Or maybe adventures make you better. They build you."

"You're delusional, Mr. York. You'll doom yourself to a lifetime of reckless wandering and pitfalls—the same sort of thing you experienced this very night!"

"Perhaps... but perhaps that's better than a bland, pointless life... the life of a Man with No Story."

"Drink! Drink the broth, Mr. York!" Sym-Iy-Kro's voice had devolved to a hoarse whisper-hiss.

Mr. York swallowed his fear and stood firm.
"No! And, if you'll excuse me, I'll be on my way."

Sym-Iy-Kro screeched and lunged at Mr. York.
"Drink!"

Mr. York leaped back and hurled the goblet at his tormentor, and Sym-Iy-Kro recoiled with a shriek.

Mr. York paused for a split second to marvel at his own bravery, and
n he turned and fled before the fiend could come at him again.

He flew down the spiral staircase,
oring the howls and screams around
n. He scampered past the
tekeeper, kicked open the
oors, and dashed into
he outside mist.

The West Bleekport Gang had stopped a short distance from the keep to divide up their pay. The helmet-headed thief was the first to spot the escapee. He sounded the alarm with a war cr[y] that could decimate porcelain and charged, his mace cycloning through the air. Mr. York do[dged] the blow, and the villain slipped and toppled over from the weight of his own weapon.

The other thieves jumped to attention and drew their blades. Gar-face and Eel-neck rushed
r.York as one. Mr.York stepped nimbly aside, and the thieves crashed into each other and
ollapsed in a heap. The eight-legger scrambled forward, only to trip over Helmet-head's
nace and skitter into a mud patch.

Now the only obstacle between
Mr.York and his freedom was Blyme.
The thief chieftain twirled his
blade and flashed his
dagger-toothed smile.

Now where is you running
off to in such an 'urry?

Mr. York weaved to the left; Blyme foresaw the maneuver and blocked his path. He lashed out his blade, intent on beheading Mr. York.

Mr. York was saved by sheer accident: the eight-legger still struggling to right himself, clawed Mr. York's ankle with a stray limb. Mr. York blundered forward, unintentionally ducking Blyme's blade and ramming his attacker in the chest.

Blyme was bowled over; had he more of a face, it may have revealed a dumbfounded expression.

Mr. York regained his balance and took off, though not before aiming a sharp kick at Blyme. He missed his target of the dagger-toothed maw, but managed to catch the thief hard in the ribs.

Blyme dropped his blade and crumpled like a withered leaf, affording Mr. York the chance to escape in the swamp's undergrowth.

He ran with his head down to keep branches from gouging his eyes. He ignored the West Bleekport Gang's curses, which soon faded into the distance. Brambles and prickers tore his clothes and clawed his skin. Vines and roots snatched at his body and groped his ankles. He paid them no heed. The only thought on his mind was putting more distance between himself and the Northeast Edge.

He splashed through the swamp, oblivious to the mud that splattered his body with each footfall. He leapfrogged over boulders, zigzagged through thickets, and hurdled across sinkpits. He moved with a grace and speed he never would have thought himself capable of achieving.

For how long he ran? He couldn't say — fifteen minutes? Twenty? An hour? The time wa[s] a blur. His survival instincts had hijacked his brain, and conscious thought was nonexistent.

And then his feet struck solid ground. Glancing down, he saw he was back on the path. He raced along the trail, arms pumping like loose puppet limbs.

Finally he looked and saw a light through the trees. At first he figured his crazed mind was playing tricks. But *no* — the light was too steady to be an illusion. He gritted his teeth, gave one last spurt of speed, and burst from the swamp. There sat the Cankerbury Inn, forlorn as ever.

He sprinted across the clearing and pounded on the door. No answer.

"*Hello!*" he yelled. He pounded again—*still* no answer. With his remaining strength he threw his fists against the door and screamed at the top of his lungs.

"*It's <u>Me</u>, Jonathan York! Let me in, <u>Please</u>! I <u>beg</u> you!*"

At last came a familiar shuffling sound. The door creaked open, and there stood the old man. He was wearing pajamas, and his eyes were red and even squintier than before.

"Lower your voice, ya rabble-rustler! I heard you the first time!"

He adjusted his spectacles and raised the lantern. "Ohhh. It's _you_. What do you want ?"

"Sir !" said Mr. York. "I apologize for not having a story to tell earlier, but _please_ — I _must_ stay with you until daylight. You cannot imagine the horror I've been through!"

The old man scratched his chin, wiped his nose, and waved Mr. York inside. "We'll discuss it in the kitchen."

Mr. York followed the old man to the dining table. They sat at opposite sides, and Mr. Yo... began to tell the old man all that had happened to him since he'd left the Cankerbury Inn.

He told of his wanderings through Halfrock Swamp and of the charlatan C. Percival Trullus...

...he told of the Whisple Tree, the vile West Bleekport Gang and their evil leader, Phintesmo BLYME...

...he told of the treasure hunt, his encounter with the Bogglemyre, his brush with the Fear 'im Gnott, and his battle of wits with the TERRAQUEENPiN...

...he told of the SiNiSTER Necromancer SYM-IY-KRo, and how he was nearly Zombified...

...he told of his escape, his mad dash through the swampland, and then, FiNALLY, Mr. York had nothing more to tell.

The old man leaned back and patted his stomach as if he'd just finished a big supper.

"That, young Mr. York, was quite a story. Had I not lived the last three decades in Halfrock Swamp, I might not have believed a word of it."

"So you will let me stay the night?" said Mr. York. "Surely you wouldn't send me back out again, not after all I've suffered."

The old man chuckled and slapped his knee.

"No, I won't send you away, stop yer frettin'. Remember, the price for a room is one story, and you, Mr. York, have just handed me a dandy of a yarn if ever there was one."

The old man rooted through his pocket and fished out a key. Mr. York heaved a final sigh of relief and reached for it, but the old man pulled back.

"Before you shuffle off to sleep through whatever remains of this night, I do want to apologize for my earlier behavior. I suppose you think I'm an ogre for sending you away like that, and perhaps you should. But before you cast your final judgment, let me ask you this: when you're old and gray like me, and someone asks for your story what would you rather have—nothing at all, or the story you lived through tonight?

"Yes, it was horrible while it lasted, but now that it's over, you have a story I'll be telling the rest of your life. Telling to your children, to your grandchildren, and, if you're lucky enough, to your great-grandchildren. Time will take many things from you. It may take your health, your loved ones, your worldly possessions... but no matter what happens, you'll *always* have your story, and as long as you tell it, it will live on and on."

Mr. York chewed his lip in what may or may not have been earnest contemplation.

"Very well," he said at last. "I see your point.

...May I have my key now?"

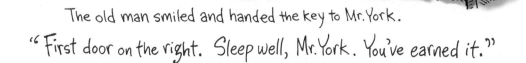

The old man smiled and handed the key to Mr. York.

"First door on the right. Sleep well, Mr. York. You've earned it."

Mr. York rose from the table and staggered down the hall. He jostled open the door to his room and flopped into bed. The springs squealed and the sheets were musty, and he wondered if all the earlier excitement would keep him from rest, but his eyelids turned to lead the moment his head hit the pillow. His thoughts scrambled, and Mr. York slipped into a deep, dreamless sleep.

He woke late the next morning with throbbing muscles and a revolting taste in his mouth. downed a quick breakfast of eggs and toast offered by the old lady, and then was on his way. saw no sign of the hooded woman, the lanky man, or the odd fellow, and perhaps that was for the best.

A pristine blue sky greeted him as he stepped back onto the path. The air was brisk, and not at all mid like the day before; the first hint that summer was closing and fall was ready to debut. e swamp seemed much less menacing in daylight —*cheerful*, even— with soothing green vegetation d glassy water. Cicadas trilled in the trees above, and in the distance a bullfrog ug-a-rummed. Mr. York kept to the trails, and the movement of walking seemed to lm the aches in his legs.

By late afternoon Mr. York had reached Springshire, and from there it was only a half-hour til he was home in Brockleport. That evening, as he savored clean clothes and a hot dinner, Ir. York made a solemn vow to never again tell of what had transpired during that dreadful night in Halfrock Swamp.

This, of course, was one vow Mr. Jonathan York failed to keep.

119

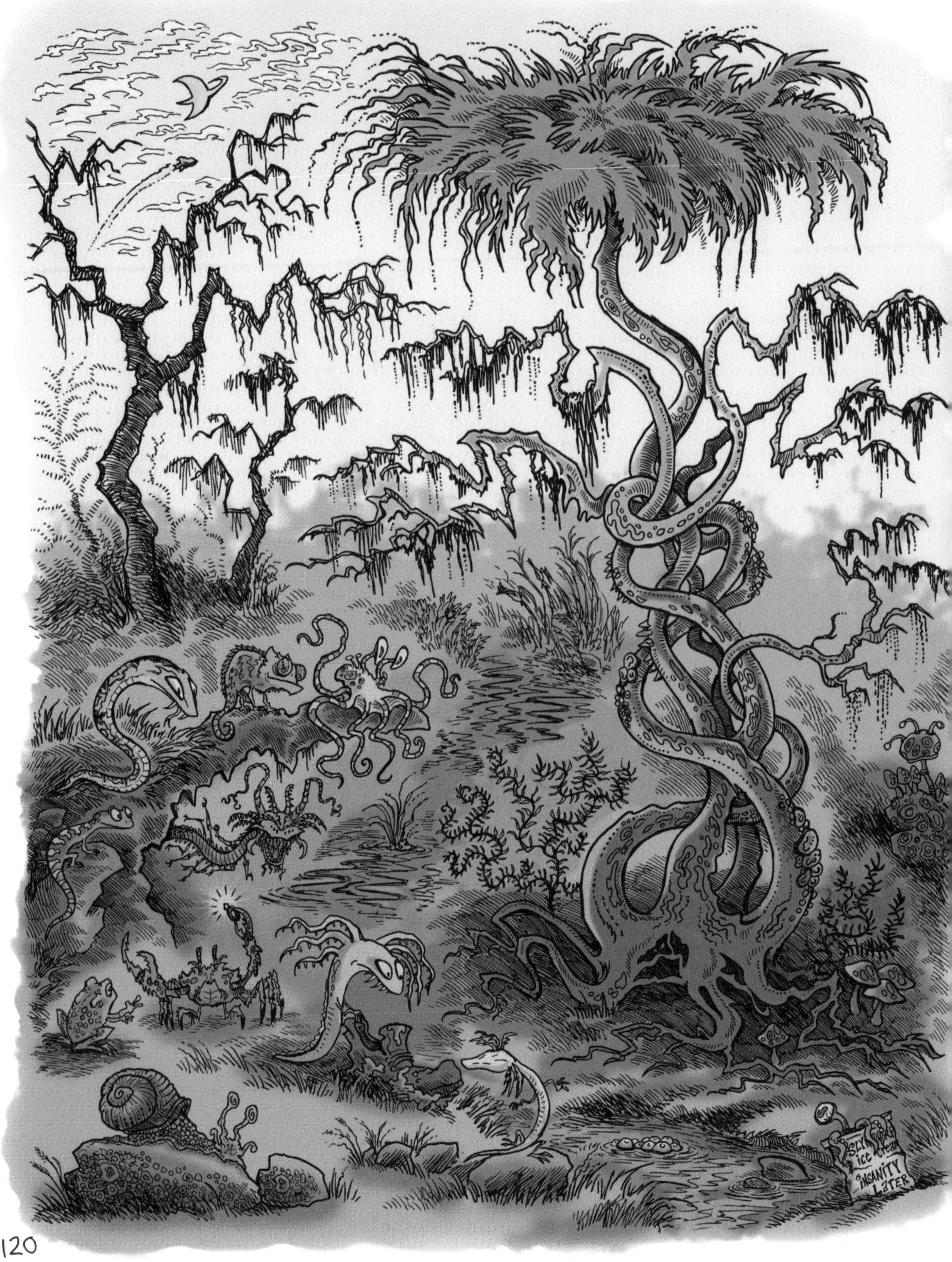
SLY
ice
...INSANITY
Later

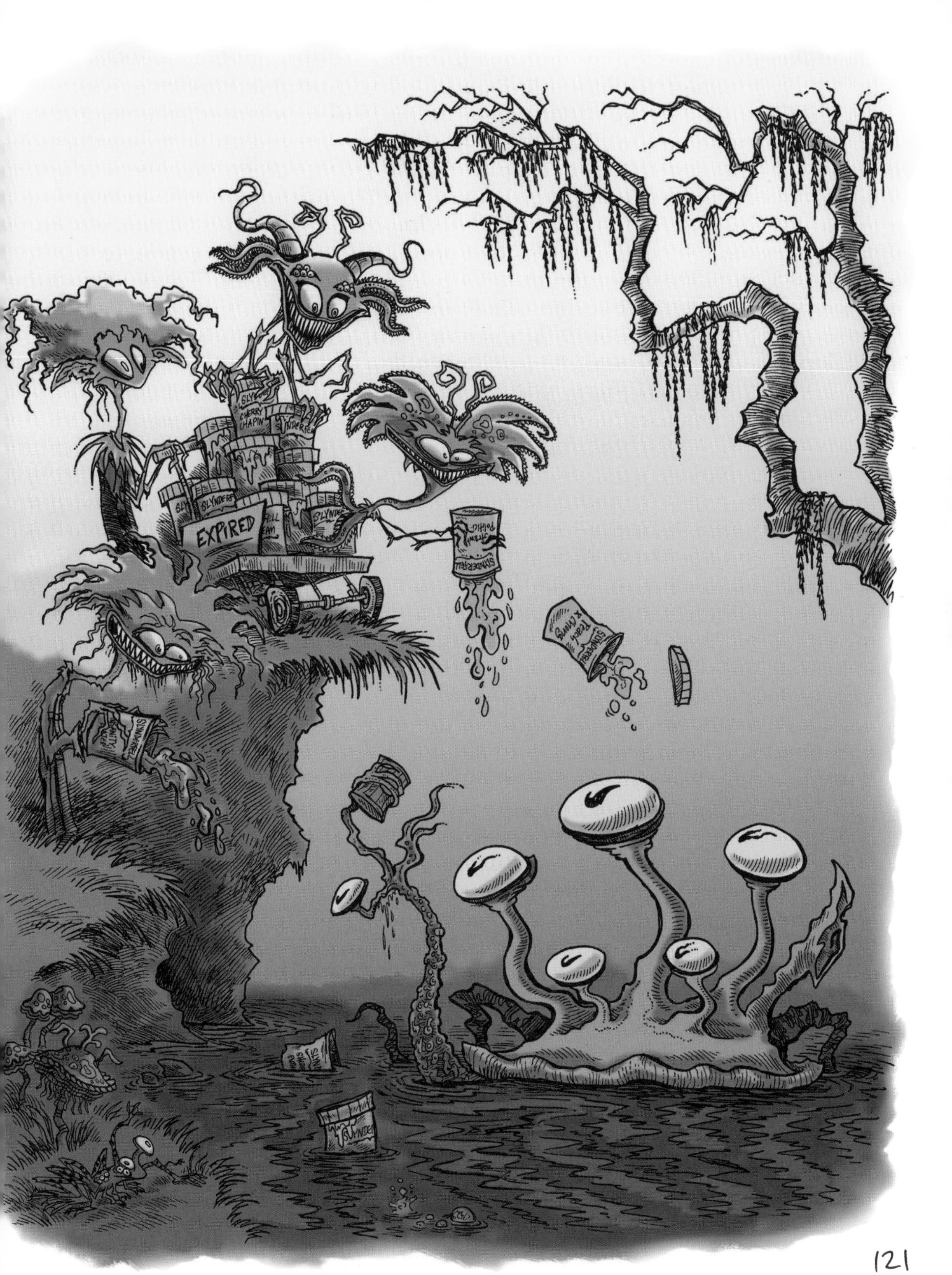
CHERRY CHAPIN
EXPIRED

"And what have we here? For me???
Ah, a tasteful offering, I deduce!
A tangible tribute to my supreme
majesty...And it's just GAWgeous!
...Pity it's not in blue."

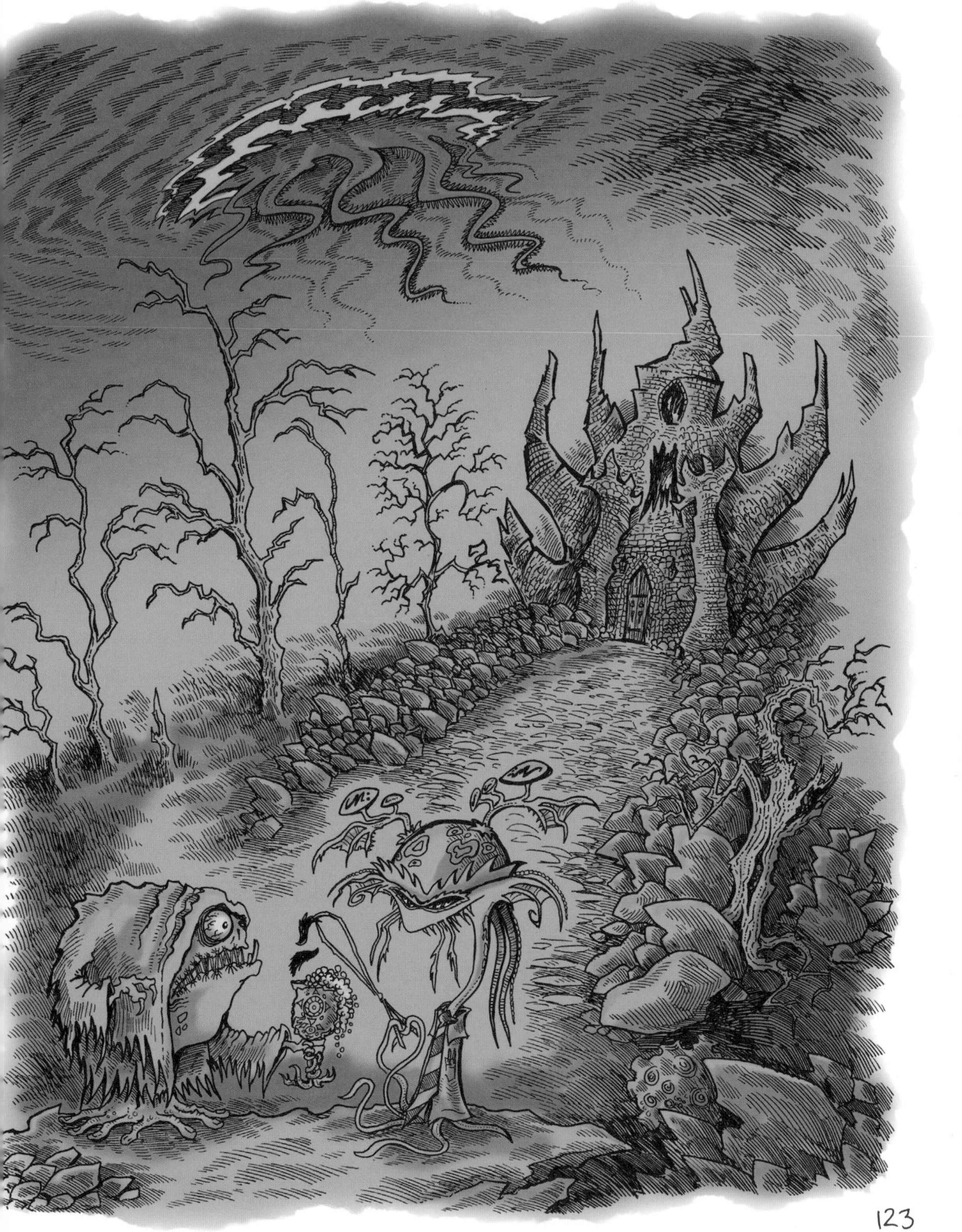

"Dat's right! Treasure beyond your wildest imagernation! All yas gotta do is go to da Whisple Tree in da swamp and knock tree times fast and tree times slow.

heH hEH Heh..."

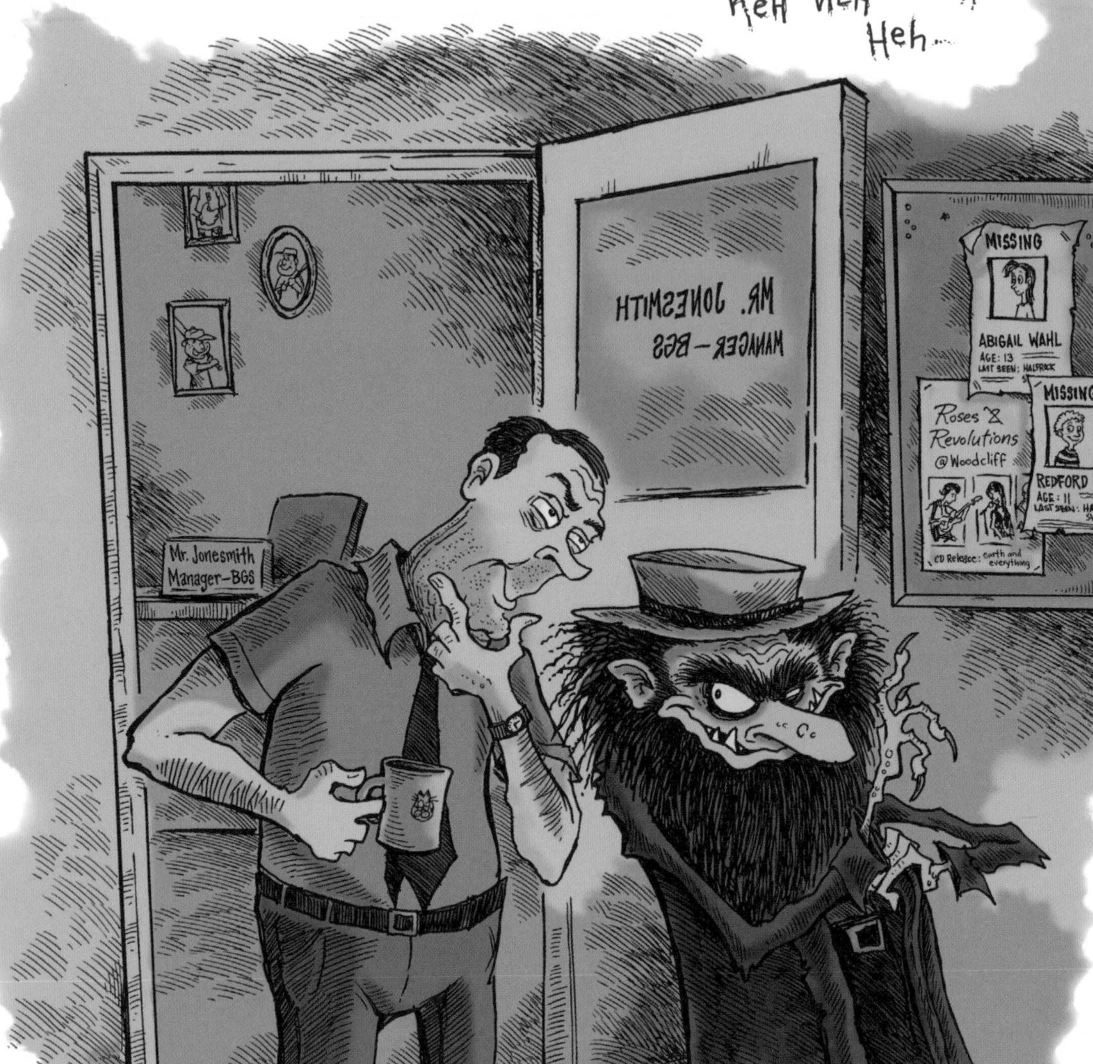
MR. JONESMITH
MANAGER—BGS
Mr. Jonesmith
Manager—BGS
MISSING
ABIGAIL WAHL
AGE: 13
Roses & Revolutions
@Woodcliff
MISSING
REDFORD WAHL
AGE: 11
LAST SEEN: HALFROCK SWAMP

The End.

a bit about the author:

By day Kory teaches K-6 Art
at a New York public school.
By night he draws weird monsters.

He is usually a very
boring person.

This is his first
published book.

Andrews McMeel Publishing, LLC
an Andrews McMeel Universal company
1130 Walnut Street, Kansas City, Missouri 64106

www.andrewsmcmeel.com

15 16 17 18 19 TEN 10 9 8 7 6 5 4 3 2 1

ISBN: 978-1-4494-7100-2

Library of Congress Control Number: 2015937245

Made by:
1010 Printing International, Ltd.
Address and place of production:
1010 Avenue, Xia Nan Industrial District,
Yuan Zhou Town, Bo Luo County,
Guang Don Province, China 516123
1st Printing – 7/13/15

ATTENTION: SCHOOLS AND BUSINESSES

Andrews McMeel books are available at quantity discounts with bulk purchase for educational, business, or sales promotional use. For information, please e-mail the Andrews McMeel Publishing Special Sales Department: specialsales@amuniversal.com.